# Felony
## EVER AFTER

**13 Authors
1 Story**

# A Note From Helena and Debra

Welcome to Felony Ever After. This process started as a wild idea over a year ago and we quickly accumulated the stunning roster of authors you will read in just a few moments. Everyone was on board for something wickedly different. The challenge was this: Pass one chapter to the next author with just the vaguest of outlines to work from and see what emerged. We were guilty of passing a box from one chapter to the next to try and mess with each other. See if you can find out who finally had to handle what was in it.

We wanted to thank our fellow authors for the chance to collaborate on such a unique project. We all have to give Jessica Royer Ocken a round of applause because she is the most amazing, flexible editor in the world. CP Smith is a dream formatter, and sitting at the computer for days at a time working with two crazy authors is something she was willing to commit to. A quick boob tap to Teresa Mummert for being on standby as well. SM Lumetta's cover work is our favorite, and gratitude belongs there. High tits for Nina Bocci and her magical PR expertise. Huge love and appreciation to Sarah Piechuta and Mr. Anastasia for proofing this insanity faster than a lightning strike and to all the authors involved who jumped on the brain train with us.

So please enjoy, in this mix we have Wall Street Journal, New York Times and, USA Today Bestsellers, Amazon rock stars and a fabulous handful of debut authors cutting their teeth on this wild adventure. So let's get on with the show, here's what thirteen Indie authors can put together…

Love, Helena & Debra

# Copyright

Copyright © 2016 Hunting Anastasia Productions
All rights reserved

Published by Hunting Anastasia Productions

Cover art design by Shannon Lumetta
Cover font from Misprinted Type
Cover image from ArtMarie at istockphoto.com
Back cover image: jo_poker_Depositphoto.com
Formatting by CP Smith
Editing by Jessica Royer Ocken
Proofing by Sarah Piechuta and Eve Chin Lavin

*Felony Ever After* is a work of fiction. Names, characters, places, and incidents are all products of the authors' twisted imagination and are used fictitiously. Any resemblance to actual events, locals, or persons, living or dead, is entirely coincidental.

Except as permitted under the US Copyright Act of 1976, no part of this publication may be reproduced, distributed or transmitted in any form by any means, or stored in a database or retrieval system, without the prior written permission of the author.

# Dedication

*This is for all the readers who think outside the box.*

## Chapter 1

### Stolen Taxi
### Debra Anastasia

The pen hit the ground in front of her. It was the oldest, stupidest trick in the book. Anytime she wore a skirt, Mr. Lay would manage to "drop" an office supply. Two months into this job as the receptionist for SalesExportt.com, Verity Michaels was on to him.

"I'll be needing that." He pointed to the pen.

"Then you'd better pick it up." She twirled on her heel and walked toward the door.

Verity was still wrapping her head around her boss's unique combination of hotness and complete social ineptitude. When she'd first arrived at good ol' SalesExportt.com—a small fashion/clothing import-export business—she'd noticed that Larold S. Lay, CEO and president, was pretty attractive. But then he spoke. Or moved. Or interacted in any way with the people around him. His personality was off-putting. And this helpless act seemed to be his version of flirting.

*Thank God it's Friday. Just a few hours more.*

She'd almost reached the door to leave his office when he thought of something else to say.

"How's the report about the certified pre-owned jeans coming?" Suddenly he was all business. "I trust you're getting it together?"

"You'll have it next Thursday. Like you asked," she reminded him. But she'd lost the battle.

"I like to be timely. Of course you know that." He waltzed up to his pen and grabbed it with as much defiance as he could muster. He also managed to take a peek at himself in the reflection of the office's tinted window.

Verity stared at him for a moment. He was a manufactured and manicured kind of handsome. His five o'clock shadow never took a break, his pants were never wrinkled, and his white smile was chemically blinding. His attention had been flattering and a little exciting until Verity realized just how weird he was—and that she was one in a line of plenty anyway. For some of the women around the office, his good looks and impressive title were enough to get past the rest, it seemed. But Verity was determined to succeed because she worked hard and earned it, taking a pass on sleeping with her creepy boss so she could make her father proud.

"It's like his last name's a prophecy." Angie Bobshell, head of sales, had rolled her eyes while dishing with Verity at the end of her first week of work. Apparently receptionists at SalesExportt.com usually did better if they were young, tight, and willing.

Verity shook her head, hoping her disgust wasn't evident on her face. "You know what, Mr. Lay? I think I'll get started now."

"Are you sure? I'd love to take you for a drink. You can tell a lot about a woman by what she orders." Lay seemed to be trying to bulk up his pecs as he spoke, making his voice sound strained.

Verity left Lay's office and stomped down the hallway to the elevator, which would take her back to her desk one floor below. Though the company was small, Lay had arranged the offices over two floors in the Bunts highrise, which was near the Chrysler Building in Midtown Manhattan. Made things more impressive, he'd explained during her interview.

The worst part was, he *had* a secretary. But Marge was way past retirement age and left when she wanted. She was more like an office cat than a worker. So all these reports that were supposed to be her responsibility had somehow become part of Verity's job. She realized she stayed late to work on them a lot so she could avoid Lay's drink offers on his way out of the office. She slapped the down button like it owed her money.

It *was* all about money. Her paycheck here was the best one of her life. Her father had arranged the job interview for her after discovering Mr. Lay belonged to the same college fraternity. Totally different generations, but just uttering the three Greek letters inspired an involuntary, elaborate handshake and an immediate desire to do favors. And who was she to refuse? She'd been in the dog house with her father after her attempt at a photography business was a complete flop in her small Florida town. He had given her the seed money that evaporated in the process.

After she'd spent a few months wallowing in yoga pants, he'd dared her to try for a job in NYC—a "real job" in the business world, he'd specified. He'd paid for the trip, as well as arranging the interview, but now she was on her own. It was a little bit thrilling, but most of the buzz of getting the job and moving to the big city had worn off when she'd had to sell her beautiful camera to afford the security deposit on her tiny apartment.

With startup expenses out of the way, Verity hoped to kick ass at work, keep earning that fabulous salary, and eventually save enough to buy her camera back. Even if photography couldn't be her job, she wanted it in her life.

Settling back at her desk downstairs, Verity pulled up the report Lay had drafted. It would take at least two hours to translate the talk-to-text nonsense he insisted was coherent.

He came down the elevator not even ten minutes later, talking loudly into his phone, set on speaker, as usual. He didn't acknowledge her on his way out, which was shitty but kind of a blessing.

"Son of a bitch." Verity typed as fast as she could, but beefing up Lay's weak sentences took her way past the time she felt comfortable on the train. So she'd be paying for a cab to boot.

It was almost ten when she finished, but now it was done—and done well. Verity dropped the report on Lay's desk, and the security guard walked her out the building's front doors and locked them tightly behind her. The cab he'd called for her pulled up as she stepped onto the sidewalk. As she approached, a sketchy-looking guy wearing a hoodie trotted up and held the car door open for her.

"Share the ride? Where you headed?"

The last thing Verity wanted to do was sit beside a tattooed druggie. But she smiled, deciding to be polite.

"Forty-third between Ninth and Tenth." *Please be going the other way.*

"Perfect. Get in." He motioned for her to enter.

Verity worked at not giving him knowledge of her panty color as she climbed in and slid over. She told the cab driver her address in Hell's Kitchen, and he nodded as she pulled out her phone to tweet. It made her feel less alone in this huge city. It also gave her a way to look busy. Surely that, combined with the taxi's annoyingly loud music, would keep Tattoo quiet.

"Boss keep you late?" he asked.

*Or not.*

"More or less. He's a real prince." *Don't dis the boss, you ninny. This guy's probably his brother.*

"Tough. You headed home to the husband?"

She slid her gaze to his face. The first thing she noticed were his blue eyes. Second, he wasn't checking out her cleavage, just waiting for her answer. And the question seemed flirty, but his face was earnest.

"We getting personal here? I'm sharing a cab with you, not filing joint taxes." She crossed her legs and was knocked off kilter by the cabby's erratic driving. She steadied herself on the door handle. She hated touching anything in a cab.

The tattooed guy shook his head and smiled, not pressing her further. He started drumming his hands on his thighs. Probably cracked out on something. He had his hood up and a beanie pulled low on his forehead.

The cabby cursed as he pulled into a traffic jam. He tried to merge into a faster lane and cut off a Mustang to do it, though it got him nowhere. The Mustang's driver was huge and filled to the top with road rage. He hopped out of his car like the cabby had slapped his mother with a dead chicken.

"Oh, shit," the tattooed passenger observed.

The cabby, God bless his crazy ass, was just as insanely angry as Mustang. He leaped out the door and the two men went toe to toe, letting the insults fly.

Verity was trapped between the fight and Tattoo. "What are we going to do?" she wondered aloud.

A green light loosened the traffic enough that the cab and the Mustang were now obstacles in the flow. Mustang Rage Monster tossed the cabby against Verity's door. She reached over and hit the lock.

Her fellow passenger opened his door, hopped out, and re-entered in the front seat. He scooted over behind the wheel and threw the cab into drive.

"Buckle up, baby!" Tattoo calmly drove the cab through the green light, leaving the two men fighting in the center of the street.

Verity turned to see them quit their fisticuffs to watch the cab pull away.

"Are you stealing this cab? Right now? With me in it?"

Despite the fact that he was now technically a felon, Tattoo drove very carefully.

"No, I'm removing us from a dangerous situation. That cab driver entered a verbal contract to get us from point A to point B. I'm just helping him fulfill his duties." Tattoo winked at her in the rearview mirror.

Verity covered her mouth for a minute while she tried to register what was actually happening to her. *Am I being kidnapped? Murdered?*

Tattoo changed the radio station, and one of her favorite songs came over the speakers.

"Great tune!" He tapped on the steering wheel.

According to the meter, they now owed the non-existent cabby twenty dollars.

"I'll have you know that I'm carrying a taser and have a throbbing, super-contagious rash. Right now. In my pants." She pointed at the reflection of his gorgeous eyes in the mirror.

"Sounds like you have an exciting evening planned."

"Don't be a wise ass, Tattoo." She tried to estimate how slow the cab would have to be going before she could roll out of it and survive.

"Tattoo?"

"That's your name in my head right now. I'm calling the police." She looked up from her cell and she realized he'd pulled onto 43rd between 9th and 10th.

"Which building do you need?" He turned his head a bit.

"That one. The one with the brown brick."

He double-parked and got out of the cab. He opened her door before she could figure out how to unlock it.

She got out slowly, watching his hands, anticipating a trick.

"You're really high strung, Country Girl."

Verity frowned at his nickname. "Really?"

He pulled out his wallet, tossed the fare in the front seat, and closed the door behind her before following her to the sidewalk.

"What? You're Country Girl in my head right now." He clicked his tongue and smiled, revealing two goddamn dimples.

"How can you be so sure I'm from the country?" She made sure she was more than an arm's length away.

"Hmm. The taser-powered rash was a dead giveaway." Tattoo put his hands in the pockets of his hoodie. "And that southern accent is charming." He winked at her.

"I'm from Florida. I have no accent. So you're just going to leave it there? The cab?" She pointed at the distinctive yellow car.

"If that angry cabby was paying attention when we gave him our addresses, he'll know where to find it. This your place?" He pointed at her building.

"Well, yes, but—hey, wait. What if the cabby remembers where I worked?" Verity knew she was going to jail tonight. Jail would break her. "I'm getting arrested! They'll do body cavity checks."

"That head of yours went from working to jail in the span of a few seconds?" He smiled at her. Again.

"Screw you, Tattoo. I bet you've been to jail a hundred times. I never want to pee in front of a group. Ever." She walked up the stairs toward the building.

"Because I have tattoos? You're judging me on my ink?" He unzipped his jacket, letting her see the tattoo creeping up his neck.

"I'm judging you on your felony—the one I was a party to tonight." She pulled her keys out of her purse.

"Okay, that's fair. But maybe I was saving you." He bowed at the waist. "Sometimes white knights have tattoos, princess."

Before she could respond, he was off.

Her heart pounded. What a ride home. The arousal she felt was due to adrenaline, she told herself. It had nothing to do with picturing where exactly on his body his tattoos might end.

*Felony* Ever After

**Verity Michaels** @VerityPics03
If my boss tries to see my cooch one more damn time, I'm putting hot sauce in his coffee. #EyesUpHere

**Verity Michaels** @VerityPics03
Oh, how did you get home tonight? "The usual. Felony combined with crazy." #NeverAgain (TwitterPic)

**Verity Michaels** @VerityPics03
Okay, a guy with a neck tat can be sexy, right? That's allowed? #ReplacingBatteriesInTheRabbit

Pandora's Box
J.M. Darhower

On Monday morning, Verity was late.

She *hated* being late.

She hated anything to do with tardiness—hated it even more than she hated taxicab-thieving tattooed dudes.

Ugh, okay, so she maybe didn't *hate* taxicab-thieving tattooed dudes. Well, not *all* of them anyway. Just the one that had gotten up in her head all weekend long. That one was the reason she was running almost thirty minutes late for work. Never in her life had she slept through her alarm, but in the midst of a particularly hot and heavy dream, she'd ignored its noise. The obnoxious beep-beep-beeping got lost somewhere with the phantom bang-bang-banging of a headboard in her subconscious and her neighbor angrily beating on their shared apartment wall, trying to get her to turn the damn alarm off.

There was no time for the subway. No, she'd have to rush and take another cab to the office. Thankfully, this one wasn't stolen.

At least, not while she was *in* it.

"You're late."

Those words slapped her in the face as she skidded to a stop in front of her desk, almost colliding with an immaculately dressed Mr. Lay. *Ugh.* He stood there, staring at his expensive watch, almost as if he'd been waiting for her.

Verity nervously smoothed her dark hair and fixed her black pencil skirt, trying to pull herself together. "Yes, I, uh...well, you know..."

She stammered for an excuse, but it was pointless. The man wasn't listening to her anyway. His eyes drifted from his watch straight to her chest. In a rush, she'd thrown on a white blouse, tighter than she liked for work, and given no thought—until now—to the black bra she wore beneath. He was practically eye-fucking her tits through the material.

"It's unfortunate," she muttered, crossing her arms over her chest. "But I'm late."

His eyes raised to meet hers, a glazed look on his face—as if he could see her standing there, all right...just with less clothing on. *Pig.*

Verity stepped past him to her desk, willing the phone to ring for an easy escape from his bullshit. But he cleared his throat, and the phone remained stubbornly silent.

"I'm expecting a package," he said. "It should've been here already."

She looked up to find him checking his watch again. "An important one?"

"Yes. A personal one. And an important one." Lay looked suddenly nervous and adjusted his necktie awkwardly. He swallowed before checking out his reflection in the tinted glass behind her.

Verity tamped down the desire to roll her eyes. "I'll be on the lookout for it."

"I know you will," he said, striding toward the elevator. "After all, we all want to be good at our jobs." He smiled as if this were a great secret they'd shared before adding, "Though we certainly could pay you to be a decoration. You look great today."

Verity scowled, mentally flipping him off for that comment, but he scurried into the elevator and was gone.

"Whoa, whoa, whoa—back up here. The guy stole a *cab*? Like, a real cab? Are you kidding me? I'm out of town for one lousy weekend and shit gets crazy!"

Angie's eyes were wide as she stared from her perch on the corner of Verity's reception desk. Verity nodded slowly, slouching down in her chair. Angie had strolled in a moment earlier—clearly not one to be distressed about being late—clutching a coffee and looking like she'd stepped off a Paris runway before strutting straight here. She'd made it no farther than reception, which was often the case. A love of shoes and the deviant little sparkle in Angie's eyes had drawn them together as close friends in just a few weeks.

Angie was beautiful, like the Barbie to Mr. Lay's Ken, except they got along about as well as Tom and Jerry. When she'd first come to the company, Angie said Lay had pursued her. But she'd put him in his place, and after a while, he'd stopped chasing. He seemed to know it was a game he wasn't going to win. This gave Verity hope that as soon as the shine wore off her apples, he'd move on from her as well. Too bad she didn't have the luxury of putting it to him bluntly like Angie had. Sometimes she worried he took her efforts to do good work as efforts to please *him*.

Angie was always full of gossip, but today Verity was the one with a story to share. She'd been more than happy to spill the details about the gorgeous tattooed idiot who'd jumped in her cab on Friday when she left work. She felt like a real New Yorker… sort of.

"Well, I mean, he didn't *steal* it so much as borrow it. Without permission. So whatever. I guess he stole it."

Angie shook her head. "Who does that?"

*Damn taxicab-thieving tattooed dudes.*

"So what did you do?" Angie continued. "Jump out? Scream? I would've screamed."

"I should've," Verity replied. "He was clearly crazy. I threatened to call the police before he got any bright ideas, like trying to murder me. Or, you know… *pillage* me."

He hadn't, of course. Hadn't even given any indication it was something he'd be interested in doing. But that hadn't stopped her mind from suggesting it all damn weekend long. She could still practically feel the adrenaline pumping through her bloodstream, pulsing through her body, settling right in that sweet spot between her thighs.

The sweet spot she'd told him was diseased and taser-guarded when her panic set in. *What the hell is wrong with me?*

"And what did *he* do?" Angie pressed, sipping her coffee.

"Kick you out before you could report him to the police?"

"He drove me home," she said. "Then he left."

"Then he left?" Angie's voice was incredulous. "That's it?"

"Yup. Left the taxi in front of my building."

"Seriously, who does that?"

*Tattoo does.*

Angie was still shaking her head when the phone rang. Verity picked it up, bringing the receiver to her ear. "SalesExportt.com. Verity Michaels speaking. How may I help you?"

Over and over, again and again. Verity was constantly saying those words. She fielded three calls back to back, taking messages and directing them upstairs. Angie still lingered, steadily sipping her coffee and trying to slip in more conversation between calls, but the phone wasn't being very cooperative.

The fourth time it rang, Verity snatched it up, sighing. "SalesExportt.com. Hold, please." She pressed a button before lowering the phone to her chest, glancing at her friend. She started to speak when the elevator dinged and Mr. Lay appeared in the office lobby again.

Twice in one hour. Had to be some sort of record.

He looked their direction, lips twitching with a grimace for Angie before his eyes settled on Verity. "That package show up?"

She held her hands up, still clutching the phone. "Nothing yet."

"It was supposed to be here almost an hour ago," he said, shaking his head. "That's what I get for taking a risk on a new courier."

"New courier?" Verity's brow furrowed. In the time she'd been there, they'd had the same bike messenger every day. The woman was not only punctual, she was young, and blonde, and gorgeous. Right up Lay's alley. "What happened to the other one?"

He cleared his throat. "We parted ways."

*Ah.* The unspoken message was clear, but Angie muttered the words anyway. "Lay strikes again."

He didn't stick around to respond to that, instead hitting the elevator button to head right back upstairs.

"Must be an important package," Angie mused.

"He said it was. He said it was personal."

"Probably sex toys," she said. "He's anxious for his collection of tentacle porn to get here. *Taken by the Sea Monster,* Volume 69."

Verity grimaced. "Gross."

Angie laughed, pushing away from the desk and strolling over to the elevator, still in no hurry to start her day. "Catch you later, V. I should probably go do some work before Lay finally gets the balls to fire me."

As soon as she was gone, Verity brought the phone back to her ear and hit the button, taking the call off of hold. "Thank you for holding. Verity Michaels speaking. How may I help you?"

Nothing. Line was dead. *Great.*

But more calls flooded in. People stopped by with things they needed done. Verity was drowning in unwanted interaction. She slipped away from her desk about an hour later, practically running to the bathroom to get a moment alone. It was only a moment, though, before she could hear the phone ringing again in the distance, and she heard a voice calling from her desk.

"Yo! Knock, knock! Anybody home?"

Cursing to herself, Verity slipped back out of the bathroom, nearly colliding with someone standing *right there*. Gasping, she took a step back, starting to apologize when she glanced up and saw the face.

*The* face.

His face.

A face that had hovered just above her all weekend long, there every time she closed her eyes. Those gorgeous blue eyes, the dimples, the ink that covered his skin and disappeared somewhere her subconscious was damn anxious to follow. She blinked a few times, shocked. It had to be another dream, right?

*Oh, crap. Did I fall asleep at my desk?*

Squeezing her eyes shut, she opened them again after a moment, and through the haze she still saw him standing there. No way. Reaching up, she pinched herself on the arm. "Ow!"

His smile faded to confusion. "You okay there, Country Girl?"

He was talking. Why was he talking? The Tattoo of her dreams kept his trap closed. In a snap decision, she reached over and poked him in the arm, too. He flinched with surprise, taking a step back. "What the hell?"

*Oh God.* He was real. He was really there. The phone was still ringing, but Verity barely heard it. Adrenaline surged in her again at the mere sight of the guy. Her skin tingled with something that felt damn close to excitement.

"What are you doing here?" she hissed. "Are you following me? Are you *stalking* me? I still have my taser, you know. I'll spray you. I will. I'll take your eyes right out."

Instead of seeming alarmed, he laughed. "I don't doubt it."

"What do you want from me?" she continued, her panic escalating. "Oh God, we're busted, aren't we? You got caught and turned me in. Are you wearing a wire?" She grasped at his chest, but it was hard to get a feel of anything because he had a messenger bag strapped around him. "I swear, I can't go to jail."

"Relax," he said, still laughing as he grabbed her hands to stop her pawing. "I'm not here about that."

"Then why are you here?"

Pulling his bag off, he unzipped it and whipped out a small box. It was plain brown and no bigger than a book, but it was packaged together with colorful duct tape. Wasn't like most of the packages they got.

"Is that for *me*?" Verity reached out to grab it, but he snatched his hand back, holding the box out of her reach.

He examined the top of the package before looking at her again. His gaze was intense.

"Depends," he said. "Do you want it?"

She hesitated. "It?"

"What I've got," he clarified. "Do you want it?"

Verity swallowed thickly, nodding. Did she want what he had? Abso-flippin'-lutely.

His smile returned, dimples showing. "Well, I hate to break it to you, but unless your name is Mr. Larold Lay, you're not getting it."

It took a second for that to sink in as Verity stared at him, completely thrown off by his presence. "Wait...the package is for Lay? *You*? You're the new messenger he's been waiting for?"

Before he even had a chance to respond, she wrenched the

package from his hand. It was light, so light she nearly crushed the cardboard the moment she clutched it. She shook the box, bringing it to her ear, but heard absolutely nothing. It was like the thing was full of feathers.

*What kind of kinky shit...?*

The box was snapped back out of her hand.

"Hey!" she protested. "My boss has been waiting for that!"

"You can't just take it," he said. "You have to sign for it first."

Verity rolled her eyes, watching as Tattoo tucked the package beneath his arm and fished through his bag for some paperwork. The phone continued to ring over on her desk, but she ignored it, taking his moment of distraction to check him out. He was almost exactly as she remembered; except somehow standing here he seemed even more gorgeous—in an unconventional, felon-y kind of way. Definitely wasn't her type.

Did she even have a type? She wasn't sure anymore, but if she did, it wouldn't be him. Yet there was something about him.

"Are you checking me out?" he asked, smirking as he held out a crinkled piece of paper and a chewed-up old ink pen. "You're not very subtle, you know."

Sneering, she grabbed the pen and paper and scribbled her name on the first line she spotted. She thrust it back at him before reclaiming the package, shaking it some more. *Nothing.*

"This thing is empty," she said. "You didn't steal whatever it was, did you?"

His expression hardened a bit. "Do I look like a thief to you?"

Verity wanted to say yes, because well, he kind of did. But she shrugged instead. What the hell did a thief look like, anyway? Bernie Madoff stole billions of dollars. Tattoo certainly didn't look like *him*. "Well, you did steal a cab on Friday."

"Again, I rescued you from a crappy situation. Total white knight, remember?"

"Yeah, sure," she muttered, eyeing him again. He had on a pair of jeans that looked like they'd been through a war and barely survived. His beanie covered his hair. She wondered what it looked like... what it would feel like—you know, if she ran her fingers through it. "You don't look like a bike messenger, though. Aren't you supposed to have those little biker shorts on? And one of those plastic helmets with the chin strap?"

He looked more like he flipped around on a BMX bike for kicks than rode around the city delivering crap for a living.

"I'm afraid I'm fresh out of spandex," he said, glancing at where she'd scribbled her name on the paper, his brow furrowing. "What does that say?"

"My name."

"Which is?"

"Verity," she said. "Verity Michaels."

He repeated her name quietly, like he was trying it out to make sure it fit. After a moment, he folded up the paper and shoved it back in his bag.

"Verity Michaels," he said, shaking his head. "I don't like it."

Verity scowled. "Yeah, well, what's your name?"

"Hudson Fenn."

"How very...*river-y*."

"It makes a hell of a lot more sense than *Tattoo*." Winking, he turned away. "Tell your boss I'm sorry I was late with the delivery. My bike got stolen Friday, and the one I'm riding right now is a piece of shit."

"It was stolen?"

"Yeah, it's why I had to take that cab in the first place. I filed a report, but it's pretty much a lost cause in this city, so I'm trying to make do until I can get a new one." He flashed a smile at her. "I'm sure I'll be seeing you around, Country Girl."

He walked out the door before she could find her voice. She stared at the wall where he'd been standing a moment ago.

Unbelievable.

Shaking her head, Verity continued to ignore the ringing phone as she walked over to catch the next elevator upstairs. She went straight to Mr. Lay's office, tapping on the door and waltzing in when he told her to enter. His secretary was nowhere to be found. "Your package is here."

"About time," he said, standing up and holding out his hand impatiently. She held her breath as he took the box, waiting for him to freak out about it being empty, but he said not a word. He showed no sign of distress, as if whatever was or wasn't in the box was exactly what he'd been expecting. "Did you sign for it?"

"Yup."

"Did you give them a tip?"

*Shit.* Verity froze. She'd been so flustered she'd forgotten.

Lay laughed. "They don't deserve it anyway. Maybe that'll teach them not to be late."

She watched as he set the package in front of him on the desk and gazed at it almost lovingly. *What is it?* she silently screamed.

"That will be all, Ms. Michaels," he said. He was too absorbed to even look at her boobs before she left.

**Verity Michaels** @VerityPics03
Do multiple orgasms count if you're asleep when they happen? #NeedToKnow #ForScience #HolyCrap

**Verity Michaels** @VerityPics03
*Brad Pitt voice* What's in the boooxxxxxx?!!! #Se7en

**Verity Michaels** @VerityPics03
Really, what's in the damn box? It's starting to piss me off.

# Chapter 3

## Bee
## Vi Keeland

Hudson's tattooed hand held a fistful of her long, wavy hair as he hovered over her. He clutched it so tightly, his knuckles had started to turn white. He trailed his tongue from her collarbone up to her ear, then bit down on her lobe. Hard. The sound of his voice matched the desperation in his grip. "I'm going to bury—"

"Verity?" Mr. Lay snapped his fingers in front of her face. "Did you hear me?"

*Shit.*

"Ummm… sorry. I was concentrating on this spreadsheet." She pointed her finger to the computer screen, and immediately realized she'd been so lost in her daydream the screensaver had activated. Mr. Lay looked at the screen and back to her.

"Coffee." He dropped a fifty-dollar bill on her desk. "Black with one sugar." Taking a few steps toward to the elevator, he turned back. "And grab yourself some too. My treat." He smiled

broadly, a little too pleased with his generosity.
*Great. Just great.*

The line at Starbucks down the block was long, and Verity found herself staring blankly out the window as she waited. Last night had been another restless, dream-filled lustathon that left her dragging when the alarm went off at six this morning. If she didn't chase Tattoo out of her head soon, she'd find herself in the unemployment line, instead of the Starbucks line. She felt her cheeks heat as she thought of her blunder in front of Mr. Lay this morning. *So not professional.*

But in the next instant, she was daydreaming again. If only Tattoo was the postman instead. Then she could count on seeing him every day. Bike messengers only came when a client utilized them. Or maybe it wouldn't even be him the next time. She felt a stab of what might have been panic. And it had only been two days.

She guzzled half of her double shot caramel macchiato before even leaving the packed coffee shop, determined to get her head back in the game, and walked back toward the office with two tall cups. The straight line of fuchsia bellflowers planted in the plaza outside of the building had just started to open. She'd been watching them grow every day, patiently waiting for the bells to blossom. When a honey bee slipped inside one of the barely open flowers, she couldn't help herself. Verity wished she had her professional-grade digital Nikon on hand, but it belonged to someone else entirely now. Her iPhone would have to do.

Crouching down, she hovered as close as she could without scaring the bee away and snapped a dozen pictures. She swiped through the shots, smiling to herself at the vivid colors and the angle of the little bee.

"Hope you're not slacking at your job…"

For a second, Verity wasn't sure if the raspy voice was real or she'd slipped back into her daydream until she felt his warm breath on her neck. Then everything became like a bad sitcom.

Verity startled, teetering back and forth before she lost her footing and tipped forward. Her phone slipped from her hand and collided with the purple bellflower. The bee that had been peacefully sipping the nectar was not happy about being disturbed and became angry. Very angry. It flew into Verity's mass of dark waves, which she proceeded to swat at like a madwoman. She stood, jumping around like, well, a girl with a bee about to sting her—and dropped her coffee just before she smacked the bee against her skin. Unfortunately, she hit him a millisecond too late, since he'd already stung her neck.

"Ouch! Oh my God! It bit me!"

"Stung, not bit."

"Who cares! Whatever it did, it hurt."

"You're not allergic are you?"

Verity became nervous. She very well could be allergic. She was allergic to so many other silly things. Tree nuts, grass, pollen, cockroaches. Why did they even test for cockroach allergies? Does anyone really need to know they are allergic to that? I mean, it's not like anyone actually thinks, *Hmmm… I'm not allergic; I'll keep this one as a pet.*

"I don't know. I've never been stung before."

Hudson pulled her hand away from her neck and leaned in. "Doesn't look any different than a regular sting."

"What are you, a bee sting expert?" Verity scowled.

"I'm just trying to help."

"Yeah, well…" She bent and picked up her phone and her

now empty coffee cup from the cement. At least she hadn't kicked over Lay's coffee when she flailed all over the place thanks to the bee, just her own. "You've helped enough today."

"What were you doing down there anyway?"

She smoothed her skirt and wiped away imaginary dirt. "I was taking a picture of a bellflower with the bee on it."

"Well, did you get it?"

"Get what?"

"The picture."

She remembered the beauty of the shot she'd captured, and it softened her mood. "Yeah, actually I did."

Hudson held out his hand. "Let me see."

She hesitated, but eventually offered him her phone. He swiped through slowly. "These are great. This one would make a kick-ass tat."

He was right. The picture he'd stopped at was the best one and would look incredible on the right person's skin. Maybe someone with smooth, tanned skin… and some tattoos that ran up his neck.

"Listen. About the other day—" Verity began. "I'm sorry. We keep a fund for tipping messengers, and I forgot to give you yours. I didn't realize until after you left."

He shrugged. "That's okay. Maybe I'll take this as a tip— with photo credit, of course." He punched a bunch of numbers into her phone and hit send before handing it back to her.

"You sent yourself the picture?"

"I like it."

She smiled and shook her head. "I better get back. Mr. Lay is going to have my ass if I hand him cold coffee."

"Mr. Lay is going to have your ass? Sounds like you offer a

wide array of reception services."

"Are those for me?" She pointed to the brown boxes in his bag.

"You want my package, don't you?" He wiggled his eyebrows.

Verity walked toward the building and entered the revolving glass door. Hudson jumped into the small compartment with her, following close behind. Simple door etiquette dictated waiting for your own compartment to swing around. Apparently no one gave Hudson the memo. Even in the elevator, he stood a little too close. She wasn't sure if he was actually invading her personal space or she was imagining things—the way she'd imagined him invading *her* last night. She shook her head and walked around her desk, forcing some space between them.

She signed for the two packages, and this time she remembered to tip him. The phone rang as she handed him the clipboard and cash. "SalesExportt.com. Verity Michaels speaking. How may I help you?"

The caller rattled on about something or the other, but Verity was too engrossed in watching Angie approach and size up Hudson to understand. Her friend licked her painted red lips as she arrived at the desk.

"Can I help you with something?" Angie asked.

"Nah. All good." Unlike every other man on the planet, Hudson's eyes didn't bulge as he got a look at Angie. He scribbled something on the delivery confirmation sheet and ripped it from the pad. "Have a good one," he said as he set it on the desk. He left before Verity could get the caller off the phone.

"Who the hell was that?" The receiver wasn't even away from Verity's ear yet when Angie started to pepper her with questions. "Did you see his ass in those jeans?"

"That's the guy I told you about the other day."

"What guy?"

"The one who stole the cab while I was in it."

"*That* was the guy? You failed to mention the most important part: He's seriously hot."

Verity shrugged, trying not to let her interest in Hudson show. Although she wasn't sure why she wouldn't admit she thought he was good looking. Just then, Mr. Lay saved her from having to discuss it much more.

"Thank heavens." He almost ran from the elevator and reached for his tall coffee. He peeked at Angie over the brim as he drank from it, dribbling a bit on his tie. Now *that* was the usual reaction men had around her. Not the non-reaction Tattoo had.

When Mr. Lay didn't seem interested in returning to his office, Angie decided it was time for her to go. "Drinks after work tomorrow tonight?" she asked as she backed away.

Lay leaned over on the reception desk like he was part of their knitting circle, wiping at his tie and nodding.

Angie waited for an awkward minute until Lay backed away from their conversation and reluctantly hit the elevator button. When the doors closed behind him, she shook her head. "How does that man even manage to get his pants on in the morning? I've never seen someone so oblivious to social clues in my life."

"I'm in for drinks tomorrow," Verity said. "Hopefully I can get out of here on time."

Angie looked at the elevator Mr. Lay had disappeared into and then back to Verity. "Doesn't matter. Just buzz me when you're on the way. I told a friend I'd meet him at the Library Bar near Columbus Circle."

The phone rang, and Verity nodded to Angie as she ducked into the elevator. When things quieted down after a string of calls, she finally noticed three things piled at the corner of her desk: The delivery confirmation, a bright purple bellflower, and the five-dollar tip she had given Hudson. He'd written two words in the corner of the invoice and signed it with an H. *Lucky bee.*

The next afternoon as Verity walked back from lunch, she looked over at where she'd fallen yesterday. "What the—?" She actually said the words out loud. The uniform line of bellflowers on the left side of the plaza was completely gone. The right side appeared intact.

She shook her head and continued inside, but her steps slowed as she got closer to her workstation. On top of the reception desk—her desk—was a vase full of vividly colored bellflowers. The same flowers she'd photographed outside yesterday. "What the—?"

As she moved around to sit at her desk, she noticed a package. It must have been delivered while she was at lunch. It was bigger than the last one, but the colorful duct tape was exactly the same. And when she lifted it, the thing was again light as air. She shook it, and just as she brought it to her ear, the elevator doors slid open to reveal Mr. Lay. He glowered at finding her investigating the box. He said nothing as he hastily stepped toward Verity, snatched it from her hands, and returned to the still-waiting elevator car.

After all that, she hadn't thought the day could get any stranger. But damn, was she wrong.

**Verity Michaels** @VerityPics03
He programmed his number in my phone & I'm out drinking tomorrow #Bootycall #Don'tDoIt #DoIt

**Verity Michaels** @VerityPics03
The Library Bar is located in the Hudson Hotel. Coincidence? I think not. #PoundingAtTheHudson #PoundHudson #Shit

**Verity Michaels** @VerityPics03
The box is back. What's in the damn boxes?

## Chapter 4

Crazy Girl
KA Robinson

*Eight o'clock.* The jackass had kept her working that late. Well, actually the should-be-retired Marge had decided afternoon Bingo was a job perk and left Verity to organize and print everything she'd been in charge of, but Verity felt like blaming Lay.

And he was still around for her to do so. He should have gone home hours ago, but she'd found him doing lunges in sweatpants and a tank top in the hall when she went to the copier. She'd given him a nod, and he'd given her the finger guns. Was he staying because he knew she had plans with Angie? *Ugh.*

Her (Marge's) tasks finally complete, Verity sent Angie a quick text before rushing to the bathroom to freshen up her makeup.

> We might have company tonight. Larold will not leave!

As soon as she saw her reflection, she winced. A day at work could really screw up a girl's appearance. Her hair was all over the place, probably because she had repeatedly run her hands through it in aggravation. Her eyeliner was smudged around her gray eyes. Overall, she looked like a streetwalker—and not the well-paid kind.

She sighed as she ran a brush through her hair and reapplied her makeup. She felt less than enthused with the results, but they would have to do. Angie was waiting for her. Well, Angie and some seriously strong alcohol, which was what she needed after an extended day with Mr. Lay.

Outside the building, she hailed a cab and clambered inside, grumbling as she went. This was the third cab she'd been in in less than a week, but she couldn't stomach the train at this moment. At least this driver seemed halfway civil.

She chuckled to herself, earning a wary look from the cabbie, as she imagined him in a fight. This time she would be the one to steal the cab, she thought recklessly. But the idea was laughable. She didn't have the balls to do something so crazy. She was the girl who'd just stayed three hours at work finishing someone else's job. Tattoo, on the other hand…

When the cab pulled up in front of the Library Bar, Verity paid and climbed out, her mind still on Hudson. As she showed her ID at the door, she reminded herself she had his cell number. It had been nagging at her constantly, but she'd managed to push it aside. *Not a crazy girl, remember?* But now that alcohol was entering the mix, she wondered if she'd be able to resist temptation.

Verity spotted Angie sitting at the bar with a man she didn't recognize. She waved as Verity made her way over to them.

"I was starting to wonder if you were ever going to show up," Angie said as Verity plopped onto the bar stool next to her and set her purse by her feet.

"Marge and her Bingo addiction kept me late. I had to hide in the bathroom and then sneak out to prevent Larold from following me here like a lost puppy. He was wearing sweats," she added before ordering a drink.

Angie's eyebrows soared, but Verity felt too tired to comment further as she glanced around the room. Couples on the dance floor seemed to be thoroughly enjoying themselves. Booths along the far wall had more couples stashed away inside, doing lord knows what within the shadows.

She frowned at the thought of all those leaving here in pairs tonight. They'd hail a cab, make out in the back seat—which, hello, was why she hated touching anything in cabs—and then go back to an apartment to make the walls shake.

Verity looked down at her fingers on the bar. It seemed like years since she'd seen action with anything besides her hand.

"Hey, what's that face for?" Angie asked.

"Hmmm? Oh, nothing. I was just thinking about the cruel injustices of life."

Angie laughed as the bartender set Verity's drink in front of her. It barely touched the surface of the bar before she grabbed it and took a healthy swallow. *Vodka and tonic.* That hit the spot.

"I suppose I should introduce you two, shouldn't I?" Angie motioned between the man on her left and Verity. "Verity, this is Joseph. We go way back. Joseph, this is the girl I talk about from work all the time."

"Pleasure to meet you." Joseph smiled at her and gave her a onceover, but not in a slime-ball kind of way. He seemed more curious than anything.

"Likewise," she said, studying him.

He was probably in his early thirties, with dark brown hair and chocolate eyes. He was attractive, but not someone she would stop to gawk at on the street. The fact that he was out with Angie, the queen of stunningly attractive men, surprised her. They really must go way back.

Verity slurped the rest of her drink and motioned for the bartender to make another. She could feel herself on that precipice between normal and starting to buzz. After everything that had happened lately, she desperately wanted a trip into buzzed territory tonight. Maybe then she'd get a decent night's sleep without Hudson starring in her very own porno.

As she drank, she chatted with Angie and Joseph. Still, her mind kept drifting back to Hudson. Why wouldn't he leave her brain? One of her dreams swam before her, and she instantly felt aroused. She shifted uncomfortably in her seat, hating the fact that he could get to her without doing anything at all.

Her phone was tucked away in her purse, but she could feel it calling. The alcohol flooding her system certainly wasn't helping her reason her way back to sanity. Instead she picked up her purse and rummaged through it until she found her phone. As she pulled it out, her stomach dropped, and a sick feeling came over her.

*What are you doing?* She couldn't text a strange man she'd been dreaming about for days! That was not at all her style. Also, said man would be dropping things off at her work for who knows how long. She had to be able to face him.

Resolved, she dropped her phone on the bar and picked up her drink. She sipped slowly, hoping to focus on its tangy taste rather than the tattooed man.

It didn't happen. Instead, as if acting on their own, her hands picked up her phone and clicked open her text messages. There he was, only a few texts down. Her fingers shook as she typed.

> Are you going to use my bee photo as a tattoo?

She dropped her phone as if it had bitten her. She was such a fool. She looked over to see what her friend would have to say, but Angie and Joseph were occupied posting selfies and artsy shots of their drinks on Instagram. *Whew.* Before she could stew in her own stupidity for too long, a message came through from Hudson.

> Why?

She tapped her fingers nervously against the bar before sending a response.

> Well, if you did, I'd expect some kind of compensation for my art.

She had no idea what she was saying, but she couldn't stop.

> Is that so? What kind of compensation did you have in mind?

She only wanted to keep him talking.

She bit her lip, imagining ways he could pay her back. None of them involved money. She struggled with her thoughts, trying to push them away. They weren't going anywhere.

> Never mind. I'm out drinking with friends. We'll talk compensation later.

The humping dots appeared.

> If you're out drinking, why did you text me?

Her cheeks heated at being caught vying for his attention.

> My phone made me. It held me hostage until I sent you a message.

She could envision his dimply smirk at her reply.

> Liar. Where are you?

She didn't see the point in lying. It wasn't as though he'd have any interest in joining her at the bar.

> The Library Bar. Why?

Instead of answering immediately, as he had before, Hudson didn't respond. Verity's eyes stayed glued to her screen, waiting. Nothing. Finally, after several minutes had passed, she texted him again.

> Hudson? Where'd you go?

No response came. She shifted uneasily on her stool; all her worries about texting him in the first place returned.

"Hey, are you okay?" Angie asked.

Verity jumped. She'd forgotten Angie was sitting right beside her.

"I'm fine." Verity mumbled.

"You sure? You seem kind of out of it tonight. Who were you texting?"

"No one important." Verity said, checking her phone again to make sure she hadn't missed a message from Hudson. She had.

> Turn around.

Verity slowly swiveled to look behind her. Her eyes widened when she saw Hudson standing only a few feet away.

He grinned as he approached. "Mind if I take a seat?"

Verity only nodded, unable to find her words.

Hudson sat beside her. "I bet you're wondering what I'm doing here, aren't you?"

Verity cleared her throat as she tried to find her voice. "Yes, I suppose I am."

"Well, I was in the area. When you said you were here, I had to come see for myself."

"See what?" she asked.

"I wanted to see you drunk. You're so tightly wound every time I see you. I thought you might be a little... looser tonight." He smirked.

"Are you asking if I'm loose?" Verity blurted.

Hudson laughed. "Now, why would you think that?"

"You should go," she said, ignoring his question.

He leaned forward, resting his elbows on the bar, and signaled the bartender over. "Oh, I think I'll stick around for a while. Tonight is going to be interesting."

"Why?"

Hudson only smiled, but Verity felt her underwear burst into flames. She was so screwed.

**Verity Michaels** @VerityPics03
I'm so screwed. #VodkaIsNotMyFriend

**Verity Michaels** @VerityPics03
Why didn't Angie take my phone away? #DoubleScrewed

**Verity Michaels** @VerityPics03
I wonder how far that tattoo goes... #INeedLaid

# Chapter 5

### Recognition
### Penelope Ward

After shooting a wink at her, Angie took off with Joseph to the other end of the bar to play darts, leaving Verity alone with Hudson. It was getting really hot all of a sudden.

Hudson leaned in, his breath warming Verity's eardrums. "Why do you keep messing with your phone and pretending I'm not here?" He'd donned a gray beanie and looked better than ever with his hair sticking out from under it. The gray brought out the blue of his eyes.

She put her phone back in her purse. "It's none of your business what I'm doing."

He took his own phone out of his pocket and scrolled through it. Looking up at her, he said, "You were tweeting again."

Her stomach dropped. "Excuse me?"

"By the way, if you want to know how far my tattoo extends, why don't you just ask? I'll show you."

*Fuck.*

*Fuckity. Fuck. Fuck.*

A hot flash ran through her body, and it felt like the room was spinning. "You've been stalking me online?"

"You're the only Verity Michaels in the United States. It wasn't that hard. And I wasn't stalking you. I looked your name up once, and bam—your Twitter account popped up, along with the hashtag 'pound Hudson'."

Mortified could not begin to describe Verity in this moment. She immediately got up from the bar. "Oh my God."

He gripped her arm. "Where are you going?"

"I… I need a shot of vodka."

Hudson wrapped his firm hand around her torso and guided her back to her stool. She felt the muscles between her legs clench at his touch.

"Relax. I'll get it," he said, stepping down the bar.

Verity slumped on her stool. It was hard to breathe normally as she absorbed the fact that he'd seen what she'd written about him. His back was toward her as he waited for their drinks. She loved the way his jeans hugged his ass. Angie and Joseph returned from the dart boards, proclaiming the place too busy to throw any more sharp objects, and startled her out of her thoughts.

"What's hot bike-messenger-cab-thief doing here anyway?" Angie whispered, her eyes wide.

"He's stalking me."

"Lucky girl."

"No, I mean, *really* stalking me. He looked me up online and read all of my tweets, apparently."

"What's wrong with that?"

"I basically tweeted that I wanted to fuck him. I used his

name in a hashtag."

Joseph bent his head back in laughter while Angie covered her mouth and spoke through her hand, "Oh, shit."

"Exactly."

Hudson reappeared at Verity's side with two shots of vodka, one for each of them. He raised his chin toward Joseph and Angie. "Hey. I'm Hudson."

Joseph reached out and glanced down at Hudson's tattooed fingers. He then took a closer look at him and squinted. "Don't I know you from somewhere?"

Shrugging, Hudson replied, "I don't think so."

"Hmm... I'm pretty sure I do," Joseph said, scratching his chin. "I just can't figure it out."

Angie leaned toward Hudson. "Anyway, nice to see you again."

"Have we met?"

"Yes. You deliver packages to our office. We've spoken briefly."

"Oh, my bad."

It amazed Verity that Hudson had no recollection of Angie. Even she had been impressed by the woman when they'd first met.

After another moment, Angie nudged Joseph toward a table that had opened up and waved, evidently at someone she knew. "Get it, girl," she whispered as she and Joseph walked away together.

Hudson spoke in Verity's ear. "So, back to our conversation..."

"What conversation?"

"The one about your need to get laid and desire to pound me."

"Get over yourself," she huffed. "You're really not my type."

"So, I'm good enough to fuck but not good enough to date?"

"No... I would not actually have sex with you, either."

"There's a *different* Hudson out there that you've been tweeting about wanting to pound?"

Verity's blood boiled. She looked up at the recessed lighting in the ceiling in an attempt to compose her thoughts. "Blurting something out on Twitter and actually following through are two totally different things."

"Let me get this straight. You find me physically attractive, you talk about having sex with me to hundreds of people, but you wouldn't touch me with a ten-foot pole? Why did you text me then?"

"It was a lapse in judgment." She lifted her empty shot glass. "You can see I've been drinking."

"So, you're saying you do stupid shit when you drink, and texting me is an example?"

"Basically, yes."

"Why are you being such a bitch? I don't believe that's who you really are—not for one minute, Honeybee."

"Honeybee?"

"Yes, fucking Honeybee. That's what I call you in my head now. I hate your name, remember?"

"How can you possibly know that I'm not really a bitch?"

"Someone who stops to take pictures of bees nestled in flowers can't be that cold-hearted."

"Look, I'm really not trying to come across as mean. You're just... I don't think we're compatible. So you're wasting your time."

"Because I'm a bike messenger? Is that why? You must have

some preconceived notion that I lack ambition. Last time I checked, you don't exactly need a Ph.D. to be a receptionist."

"It has nothing to do with your job."

"Okay, then. What is it?"

"It's not something I can explain. You just seem... dangerous—like someone I should stay away from."

"Dangerous," he repeated. "Okay, so you *do* like me, but that scares you because I'm different than the straight-laced guys you're used to."

"Don't put words in my mouth."

"Would you prefer something else?"

Verity's mouth dropped open. "You're insane."

His blue eyes were piercing. "You like it."

She shook her head. "I don't."

"If you didn't, you'd be long gone."

Verity sighed. She *did* like it, and this exchange was only making her hotter for him.

"What do you do, Verity?"

"What you mean?"

"Besides your meaningless job—what makes you tick?"

She let out a deep breath and decided to answer him honestly. "I like to take pictures. I'm a photographer."

"So, when I caught you taking the photo of the bee, there's more where that came from?"

"Yes. A lot more. I have—well, used to have—a professional camera and a business. I'm working on fixing things so I can dabble in photography on the weekends."

"I'd love to see your photos sometime. What do you like to shoot?"

Just thinking about taking pictures softened her. "There is

infinite material to be found in Central Park. I like to take nature shots, especially when the trees are in full bloom. But my absolute favorites are candid shots of unsuspecting people."

He wiggled his brows. "You're a bit of a voyeur."

"Not in the way *you* probably are." She looked down at her empty glass. Without asking, Hudson took it to get her another drink.

He signaled the bartender, and a few minutes later, another vodka tonic appeared.

Verity smiled. "Thanks."

"I'm capping you at this one."

"Why?"

"I get the feeling you're a messy drunk."

*Touché.*

Verity changed the subject. She didn't want to discuss her drinking and potential lack of control. "I answered your question, so what is it that makes *you* tick, Hudson?"

"Right now?" He licked his lips. "You."

She could feel herself blushing. His stare burned into her. She felt it in every nerve ending, and the fact that she couldn't control her reaction drove her crazy. Worse than being late.

Clearing her throat, she said, "I meant in general."

"I sketch custom tattoo designs for people. I really enjoy that. Ironic, considering your little nickname for me, huh?"

Verity rolled her eyes and saw Angie waving her over. She and Joseph were sitting with Marco, a wholesaler from work, and a few more seats had opened up.

Hudson escorted Verity to the table and introduced himself to Marco, saving her the trouble of figuring out how to explain him. She couldn't even explain him to herself. After a few minutes, Marco suddenly snapped his fingers. "I got it! I know why I recognize you!"

"Oh, really? You're ahead of Joseph then." Hudson said.

"You're the dude on the bike who drops off my grandmother's medicine."

"You're Edna's grandson?"

He chuckled. "Yeah."

"That's cool. Small world. She's so sweet."

Angie smiled at Hudson. "She hires you to pick up her medicine?"

"Nah. I ran into her one day when I was delivering something in her building. She was struggling to get up the stairs. She said she doesn't have the energy to go pick up her meds sometimes. I told her to call me when she's running low. She calls it into the pharmacy, and when I'm in the area, I go get it for her."

Marco nodded. "I happened to be visiting one day when he delivered them to her. Thank you, man. I know she really appreciates it."

"No problem." Hudson looked over at Verity's shocked expression and whispered, "As you can see, my dark and dangerous reputation precedes me."

Verity couldn't help but laugh. She was rather touched by what she'd heard, and felt kind of stupid for judging him so harshly. Noticing Hudson staring at her lips, she asked, "What?"

"God, you have a pretty smile."

Verity couldn't even begin to describe what Hudson's smile did to her. She certainly wasn't going to return the sentiment by admitting it. But she did need to say something... anything...

"I have to go," Hudson said abruptly, looking at his watch.

"What? So soon?" Now Verity's brain began working again.

"All of a sudden you want to me to stay?"

"Well, we were talking. I ju—"

He cut her off. "I can't stay. I have another obligation. I'm sorry."

Disappointment rushed through her. Did he have a girlfriend? Why else would he suddenly have to leave tonight?

"Uh... okay," she said, trying to sound nonchalant as she tucked her hair behind her ear.

Hudson placed his hand on her cheek and leaned in. Her heart raced because she was sure he was going to kiss her.

"Don't drink anymore. Take care of yourself," he said, just inches from her lips.

*Too close but not close enough.* When he uttered that last word—*yourself*—she noticed a shimmery piece of metal piercing his tongue.

He walked away, leaving her more aroused than she could ever remember being in all her life. She now had another fantasy to add to the list: Hudson's head between her legs as he went down on her with his decorated tongue.

Later that night, and after switching to water at the bar, she checked her email in bed before turning out the light.

*Hudson Fenn is now following you on Twitter.*

Verity clicked on his profile and noticed that it was only recently created. His profile picture was the photo she'd snapped of the bee on the flower. He had yet to send a tweet.

**Verity Michaels** @VerityPics03
I need to change my account so strange men in beanies can't find me. #Stalker

**Verity Michaels** @VerityPics03
Tell your girlfriend I said hello. #ObligationMyAss

**Verity Michaels** @VerityPics03
What's in those empty boxes you deliver??? #StillAStalker

## Chapter 6

### William Hudson Fenn
### Liv Morris

Verity woke with bright morning sun streaming through her window, as her alarm went off. She cursed the intrusion and threw the covers over her head to chase the end of her dream—a dark and delicious one that involved too much vodka and a talented tongue. Her pounding head and queasy stomach reminded her that the too-much-vodka part did happen. She hadn't switched to water quite soon enough. Her lonely bed spoke to the other.

She wondered again if another woman had enjoyed Hudson's company last night. He'd bolted out of the bar as if he'd been caught committing a crime. Someone as hot as he was had to have a girlfriend. Damn Manhattan and its lack of dateable men. Even the taken men flirted like they were on the market. Hudson's suggestive words last night lost their luster at the thought.

A couple of Advil and a strong vat of coffee later, Verity left her apartment building to face the day. Thankfully the weekend would begin in just over eight hours—unless Marge created another mess for her to clean up. The image of Larold in his sweats appeared in her head, followed by the look on his face when the last feather-light box had arrived. She shivered. Her office was a strange place.

She pressed her sunglasses tight against her face to block the blinding sun and headed to the subway with one goal in mind: find out who Hudson Fenn was. Everyone had an electronic paper trail and Vinnie, the company's IT guy, owed her a favor. It was cashing-in time.

She called Vinnie and gave him the few details she had about Hudson as soon as she'd settled at her desk, but the afternoon was nearly spent when the phone rang and she recognized Vinnie's extension. Finally. She crossed her fingers, hoping he could fill in the blanks.

"Verity?" Vinnie asked.

"Yes." She deleted the tab screen that showed her Google stalking, but the Twitter tab remained open. She'd been refreshing it all day to see if Hudson had tweeted. Nothing.

"Hey, it's Vinnie."

She danced in her seat with anticipation. Other than his Twitter profile, nothing came up under Hudson's name in the entire New York metro area. "Any luck?" She tapped her fingers against her desk as she whispered into the phone.

"I was slammed with upgrades to our system, but I was able to do some digging around." Vinnie was whispering too. "I didn't find a good match to this guy under the name Hudson Fenn. But there was a William Hudson Fenn that popped up."

"William..." It rolled over her lips in a hum. A proper

sounding name didn't fit Hudson. Well, Hudson didn't fit Hudson either. A tatted-up guy with a tongue piercing should be called Jake or Austin. "Who is he?"

"It's strange. I found that William name in an article from MIT's school newspaper. William Hudson Fenn graduated from the Institute a few years ago."

"Could it have been a typo and should've read William Hudson *Penn*? People might name their kid after a founding father, right?"

"That would make sense. I couldn't find another hit anywhere on a William Hudson *Fenn.* If the article was correct, every other record of him online has been swept clean. Sorry, Verity. I tried." Vinnie's tone indicated that his help with the search had concluded.

"I know. Thanks, Vinnie." She set down the phone and glanced up to see Angie sashaying toward her from the elevator.

Verity dismissed any possibility that Hudson had attended MIT. He worked a job that required knowing the numbers on street signs to navigate New York City on his bike. MIT grads navigated the numbers that *built* the streets.

"Hey." Angie perched her tiny self on the edge of Verity's desk. "I tried to get away before now to come talk to you. It's been one conference call after another. So your bike messengering friend showed up last night. You seemed into that. I wouldn't have thought you were a tattoo lover."

"Me either." Verity sighed and slumped back in her chair, feeling frustrated. "He's got this swagger that's hard to ignore. Believe me, I've tried to forget him all day."

Angie waggled her brows. "Those kind of men can light up the sheets."

"Don't remind me." Verity flashed back to her vodka-fueled dream. She crossed her legs and straightened up. She needed to get a grip.

"I watched the way he looked at you." Angie nodded and squinted one eye.

"What?" Verity played dumb because she didn't want to get her hopes up.

Even if Hudson didn't have a girlfriend, the men in New York seemed to have the dating attention span of a toddler at Chuck E. Cheese's. They were easily distracted in a city overrun with beautiful women—a bachelor's playground. At times she wanted to move back home and find a respectable man, but then she'd remember it was no simple task there either. Florida guys wore a lot of tank tops, and that much armpit hair made keeping a straight face on a date really hard. In NYC, at least the guys mostly wore sleeves.

"He didn't look at anyone else. He came to see *you*," Angie confirmed.

"But he left so suddenly, and I haven't heard from him since. I've been checking every four minutes since the cab dropped me off last night."

"So you were expecting him to make contact?" Angie flashed Verity a knowing smile and added a wink. "I have a good feeling about this one. Plus, he delivers packages all the time."

"Stop it. You're getting my hopes up," Verity countered. "Mr. Lay keeps coming down looking for today's package. But so far nothing's arrived."

"It's almost five. Looks like he isn't getting one today." Both Verity and Angie turned toward the elevator as it dinged, announcing an arrival.

Angie jumped off Verity's desk, clearly expecting Mr. Lay to come out of the elevator in a rush of swinging arms and weirdness. Instead, the steel doors opened to reveal Hudson Fenn—a heart-stopping, polished bad-boy version dressed in dark, fitted jeans and a black leather jacket.

Verity brought her hand to her chest with a thump.

"Wow." Angie whistled.

Verity heard her, but her voice sounded like an echo down a long tunnel. Everything else faded as Hudson's stare turned her into a weak-kneed mess. When he threw her a smirky grin, she grabbed hold of her desk. He strode toward her, and she swallowed hard at the sight of him: pure hot-rocker fantasy. When he leaned on her desk, she caught the scent of his leather jacket. She bit her lip and peered up at him.

"Did you give up on me today?" He placed a bedazzled package on her desk. Someone had sealed the box with a hot glue gun and black plastic beads. "My client was running late."

Verity reached out to examine the cardboard craziness Hudson had delivered. She gasped when she realized the black beads were actually tiny skulls. "Your client is running a little strange too." She dropped the box back on her desk like it might burn her.

"Forget my client and the box. I'm taking you out. Grab your stuff and let's go."

Dismissing her concerns about the mysterious Hudson and his possible mysterious girlfriend, Verity began pulling her belongings from her desk drawer as if someone else had taken control of her body. Hudson came around and took her hand in his. His touch was warm enough to make certain parts of her melt.

"Hold on a second." She pulled him to a stop and with her free hand dialed Mr. Lay. She brought the receiver up to her ear and waited for her boss to answer.

"This better be about a package," Mr. Lay whispered when he picked up. "I've been waiting all day, hoping you would bring it up. And place it carefully on my desk."

"It's here on *my* desk." She glanced at the package and shook off the creepo chills.

"Don't forget to tip the messenger. I don't want anyone upset today. I'm coming down. Stay there, okay?" Mr. Lay disconnected before she could respond.

"Freak show." She shook her head, and Hudson laughed.

"You'd call him something worse if you worked for him."

"I'll stick to deliveries," he said, pulling her to her feet. "And you."

Verity blushed and smiled to herself. Maybe Angie was right and Hudson did have a real thing for her. She just needed to vet him on his girlfriend status.

Hudson pushed the elevator's down button, and almost instantly the doors parted. A wide-eyed Mr. Lay stood before them.

"Ms. Michaels." Verity flinched as Mr. Lay looked her over. "What are you doing away from your desk? And where is my package?"

"Let's all relax," Hudson suggested, practically yawning with indifference to her boss. "Work day's over for me—your box delivery guy—and Ms. Michaels here."

Without another word, Verity followed Hudson into the empty elevator. As the doors closed, Mr. Lay gaped, speechless, while Angie cheered silently behind him. A definite first, for sure.

Hudson brought his lips to Verity's ear and a shiver ran through her. "He shouldn't treat someone I care for like that."

Verity could only nod, her mind jumbled from his touch and words. She tried taking a deep breath, but the elevator seemed short on fresh air. All she could smell was the warm scent of Hudson's leather jacket.

When they arrived in the lobby, Hudson guided her across the marbled floors to the building's exit. He held her close as they squeezed into the revolving door. Once they were outside, she wanted his protective arms again.

"Where's your bike?" Verity scanned the area, but didn't see a single bike.

"I've planned alternate transportation for the night."

Verity followed Hudson's eyes to a black town car. A statue-like driver stood near the car's rear door and smiled at them.

Verity spun around to face Hudson with her hand on her hip. "Did you steal this ride too?"

"I told an old friend I wanted to impress a girl tonight, and he lent me his vehicle."

*Old friend, my ass.* Verity didn't believe him for one second. No one their age had cars and drivers. Something didn't add up with Hudson. *Again.*

"As flattered as I am, are you sure about that?" Verity hesitated as Hudson tried to persuade her to climb into the car. The driver chuckled beside her, and she wondered if this entire scene was part of a hidden-camera punk.

"I promise." Hudson pulled a pouty face and begged her with his eyes. "Please, Verity. Trust me."

"Yeah, right," she huffed, but she sat down in the backseat.

This likely spelled epic trouble, yet she couldn't make herself resist. Verity licked her lips as Hudson folded into the car seat next to her. She knew he would get whatever he wanted from her tonight—with or without the fancy wheels.

"Fuckity, fuck, fuck. I'm screwed," she muttered while pulling out her iPhone. She had something to say in one hundred and forty characters or less.

**Verity Michaels** @VerityPics03
If something appears too good to be true, it probably is. #WiseSayings #SmartWomen.

**Hudson Fenn** @tatwhiteknight
Sitting next to the most beautiful woman in the world. #TooGoodToBeTrue #PinchMe

**Verity Michaels** @VerityPics03
When will men learn that flattery gets them nowhere. #EyeRolls #SweetTalker

**Hudson Fenn** @tatwhiteknight
Heading out for a "photo" perfect night. #CameraInCar #LightsCameraAction

# Chapter 7

## B&E
## S.M. Lumetta

"So where are we going, Tattoo?"

Hudson rolled his eyes, but flashed that panty-dropping grin. "Is Hudson really such a bad name? It was good enough for the river."

"There's a good inspiration. Are you chock full of crap, too?"

"Ha ha. That's the East River," he said with a wink.

"Ahh…" Verity said. "It's not a *horrible* name. I just wonder what's wrong with traditional names. Like John or Matthew—"

"Mark and Luke? I don't want our kids to be named after apostles, *Verity*."

"You're a dick." *William*. No wonder he'd ditched that part of his name… if that was even him. Verity realized she still knew zip.

"A dick you want to pound," he countered.

She growled and looked out the window. "Yep, you're charming the pants right off me, Tattoo."

"You're wearing a skirt," he pointed out. "Does that mean you're commando, Honeybee?"

Verity struggled to keep her lips from curving. "Damn you."

He chuckled, and once again her entire body was aware of him. She turned to face him, almost startling when she found him watching her. The look in his eyes was the kind of predatory hunger women dream about. And as a matter of fact, she *had* dreamed of this exact look.

Verity tried to clear her throat, but ended up making some awkward squeaky noise. "Um, where are we going?"

"Surprises, woman. I got a few of them in store," Hudson answered. "I told you, I'm trying to impress a girl tonight."

"Did you bring me along to answer your phone for you while you're impressing this mystery lady?"

Suddenly Hudson's wet-dream-inducing eyes were mere inches from hers. She was pretty confident her ovaries exploded, and she pinched her knees together. A gasp she later realized was hers seemed to echo off the leather seats; his hand was on her knee. Her bare knee. The skin there was now happily on fire. *Burn, baby, burn.*

"Verity," he said, his tone incredibly serious. And sexier, *dammit*. She watched his eyes, the pull of him so overwhelming, she wished she was, in fact, commando. "Please hold all calls."

She rolled her eyes and shoved at his chest, but she didn't try very hard. He smiled and coaxed her shoulders toward him once more. She was mesmerized by his gaze and his nearness. He kept glancing down at her lips, his minty breath breaking across her face. The sparks between them were nearly visible with his mouth so close to hers. She was ready to attach herself like a Hoover and suck his face off.

"Close your eyes, Honeybee," he said, his voice low and sweet.

Like a child under a spell, she complied. But her expectations of smacktacular lip-nastics were dashed when the heat of his gaze and his body disappeared, and the car stopped.

"Keep them closed," he instructed.

Verity huffed, more to cover her disappointment than in actual frustration with Hudson's romantic game. His responding laugh was low. No matter what he did, he kept drawing her in. The laugh, the closeness, the surprises…

"Come on," he said, his hand closing around hers. The warmth of his skin sent a thrill through her as he led her out of the car.

"This better not be some sort of *Punked* thing," she told him. "I will have you killed. I know gangsters."

He full-out guffawed. "Every time I see you, I wonder what will come out of that mouth next."

After she heard the car door close, his arm and his scent wrapped around her. Following his lead, they walked together until Verity felt grass under her feet. The breeze swirled around her, carrying scents and sounds of nature.

"Flowers!" she exclaimed. "Lots of flowers!"

Hudson turned her to face a certain way. "Open your eyes, Honeybee."

The spectacle before her took her breath away. "Oh my God," she managed. "Is this—"

"The Conservatory Garden."

"At the top of Central Park, right? I've never been here." Verity was stunned. The sun cast an orange glow through the trees and over the flowers. They stood a stone's throw from the

Three Dancing Maidens fountain.

Hudson grabbed her hand and placed an extremely expensive camera in it.

"What?!" Verity shrieked. "No way. This is a Hasselblad! I shouldn't even touch it. My life insurance wouldn't cover the cost of replacing this sucker."

He laughed and made sure she didn't drop it. "I know what it is. It was my grandfather's."

"Jesus! How could you possibly trust me with an heirloom like this? It's practically priceless." She handed the camera back to him and stepped away.

He sighed, his discomfort obvious. "He would have loved to see what kind of pictures you take with his favorite camera," he said, reverently. "I trust you."

Unable to resist how desperately she wanted to try it, Verity gingerly took the camera from his hands. She examined it, turning it over in her palms, her breath hitching.

"I just—why would you do all this for me?" she asked, gesturing to the beauty around them.

"You're wasting time," he answered with a smile. "Camera's loaded. I've got a light meter and a reflector or two if you need them. Otherwise, get to it."

She grinned and nodded, kissing his cheek before scurrying off to catch the beauty before the light sank behind the horizon. Verity was so overwhelmed with options, she almost panicked. Every now and then she would pause, remembering she wasn't here alone. Hudson would smile at her, seeming content to watch her in her element. At one point, she turned the camera on him and he turned his face away, as if embarrassed or shy. She clicked the shutter anyway. That might end up being her favorite picture of the night.

Hudson kept handing her fresh rolls of film as she spent them, and before she knew it, there wasn't enough light anymore.

"Damn," she said. "How many rolls did I use?"

"Four," he told her, beaming. "I have three more for you, if you'd like."

"But the light is gone. There's not enough sun left."

Hudson pulled out his phone and tapped a few times. The overhanging tree branches, among other things, came to life with a series of subtle lights. Verity gasped. It was almost as beautiful as the sunlight over the garden. Tears filled her eyes.

"Oh, please don't cry, Honeybee," he pleaded. "I—"

She cut him off by flinging her arms around him. "Thank you," she whispered.

"You're welcome. Hasn't anyone tried to woo you before?"

She snorted, and they both laughed, hers turning to giggles before dying out when she noticed his eyes on her mouth. Her lips parted, and he closed the distance. Soft, full lips pressed gently to hers at first, parting slightly to suck on her bottom lip. Her hands seemed to work autonomously, one threading fingers into his hair while the other white-knuckled the camera behind his back. Her daydreams and nighttime fantasies swirled in her head. She tilted her head and deepened the kiss, earning a moan from Hudson. Now that tongues were involved, she was pretty sure the functioning part of her brain had signed off for the evening.

*Don't drop the camera. Don't derp camr. Guhhh.*

By the time the kiss ended, World War III could have erupted and concluded around them, and she wouldn't have noticed.

"That, beauty, was worth the price of admission," he

whispered against her mouth. "And boy, has it worked up an appetite."

"Excuse me?" She pushed back. Her misplaced offense was hilarious to him. "How dare you." He laughed harder, obviously seeing she didn't really mean it.

"Dinner!" he exclaimed. "I'm talking about food." Taking her face in his hands, he continued. "As much as I love *dessert*, I'm truly famished. Come on, I've got a picnic for us."

A short walk under the dome of trees led to a small, candlelit table covered in an array of mouth-watering food: grilled chicken, a slew of roasted veggies, wine, cheeses… A picnic might be putting it mildly. Verity didn't know where to start.

"How did you get all of this here?" she asked.

"I know a guy who works on the inside."

"Prison?" Verity asked with wide eyes.

"No. Wow. You really jump to the best conclusions when it comes to me. I'm friends with the gardener. Inside *this* place. A friend on the inside."

"Ohhhh… That makes sense. Anyway, I'm drooling," she said, wiping her mouth. "Or did you slobber on me?"

He barked a laugh. "It's possible. You do look delicious."

She couldn't help but blush. As she took a seat, she surveyed the surroundings once again. Somehow the place looked completely different than it had when she'd been wandering, taking shot after shot. And the crazy, cab-stealing deviant she'd been fantasizing over sat across from her, behind a cornucopia of appetizing food.

"How is this all happening?" she wondered aloud. "Who are you?"

He smiled. Not mischievously or smugly, but warmly, and

maybe with a touch of sadness. "I'm exactly who you see."

She looked away, wanting to argue that he never answered any of her questions. But it seemed a bad time to pick a fight.

They ate in companionable silence for a little while, exchanging plates and tapping their glasses in toast. The food was delectable, and she wondered again how he'd arranged all this. It didn't seem entirely legal.

When they did speak, the conversation flowed comfortably. Hudson shared that his grandfather, who'd taught him how to swear properly, had been a huge presence in his life. Verity admitted she was born just outside Ocala, Florida, but was sort of enjoying the city. She'd been raised by her dad after her mom left when she was little. Hudson had always lived here, though he'd lived with his mother in Yonkers for a while after his parents divorced.

"How about school?" she asked. *Was it MIT?*

"School was boring," he answered. "Who cares?"

"But you seem to have done so well with your associate bike rider degree."

He laughed and eyed her wine glass. "Your jokes get worse with every sip."

She wanted to ask what he was hiding, but he seemed determined to keep his mystery alive. And mystery or no, this was the best date of her life, so why dispel the magic? *Don't be rude*, she convinced herself. This was at least sort of a public place… she was safe, right?

When they'd finished, Hudson stood and held out his hand to her. She took it without much hesitation and rose, pressing against him. She hadn't meant to, but he seemed to have Verity magnets under his shirt.

"Thank you for agreeing to come out tonight, Verity," he said. "Ever taken a selfie with a Hasselblad?"

"Are you kidding?"

He picked up the camera from its bag next to the table and turned them toward the lights. He fiddled with the settings for a minute before managing to hold it out in front of them with a finger on the release button.

"Say pussyfeathers!"

Verity burst out laughing. When the giggles abated, she turned to glare at him. Her intent to berate him died in her throat when she saw the way he looked at her. "Did you even look at the camera?"

"Why? I was looking at you."

Her heart flipped. "Why do you have to do that?" she whispered. "It's so hard to be cautious about you when you say things like that."

"Why so many questions?" he asked, and laid a kiss on her.

"What the hell are you doing in here?!" a voice shouted. "You're trespassing!"

Verity jumped and knocked the camera out of Hudson's hand. Luckily, it fell only a short distance to the table next to them.

"Shit." Hudson picked up the camera and grabbed Verity by the arm. "Let's go!"

"What about your friend on the inside?" she yelled.

"He must not have spread the word!" Hudson yelled back, practically dragging her along.

"Tattoo," she said, panting as they ran. "I—I can't exactly keep this up in these shoes."

"Great, we're back to Tattoo again, huh, Country Girl?"

"*Hudson*, these shoes are killing me. I'm going to break an ankle."

She could hear the guard running after them.

"We can't stop." In an insane move, he slingshotted her forward and yelled, "Jump!"

Confused and hopped up on adrenaline, wine, and his hand gripping hers, Verity just reacted. As soon as her feet left the ground, she was in Hudson's arms. And he was still running.

"Holy crap!" she yelled.

He smiled, and before she knew it, they had passed the gate and were out on the street. Half a block down, the car that had brought them waited, a door open.

"I trust you enjoyed your time at the garden, sir," the driver said, calmer than a funeral director.

Verity watched Hudson wink as they threw themselves in the back. Seconds later, the car was in motion.

"So, did you like it?" he asked.

Shell-shocked, Verity stared at him. "What the hell just happened?"

"Seems my man forgot to convey the plan to the rest of the staff. Sometimes you live life on the fly." He shrugged. "Don't tell me it wasn't kind of fun getting caught like that."

"You're a total criminal, aren't you?" she asked, but to her surprise, she was grinning ear to ear.

He shook his head. "Have I stolen your heart yet?"

That stopped her cold. She blinked several times. "What?"

"Don't answer," he whispered. "I won't take it until you give it freely."

**Verity Michaels** @VerityPics03
Strangest first date ever. #SmoothCriminal #KissMeAgain #WhyPussyfeathers

**Hudson Fenn** @tatwhiteknight When someone says FIRST date, that means they want more. #IWantMore #Honeybee #BecauseILikeToMakeHerSmile

# Chapter 8

#OhDamn
Tijan

"My niece set up my Twitter account over the weekend."

Those were ten words Verity *never* thought she'd hear from Larold Lay, and now that she had, she wanted to sink down in her chair and disappear through the floor. She eyed the ground and nudged the carpet with her foot. Nope. It wasn't moving. There was no chance she could be swallowed back down to her desk. She looked up at her boss. He leveled her with a hard stare, eyebrows pinched together and mouth puckered like a confused duck.

He wasn't going away either. This bitch was happening.

Verity let out a sigh and folded her hands into her lap. "Did she? I wasn't aware you had a niece."

He cleared his throat and tugged at his collar. "Well, I have to admit I don't see her as often as I should, but her mother decided last weekend that Mexico was calling her name. She has a weakness for gentlemen named Jose, if you get my drift."

*Ah. Splendid.* Verity's lip twitched. She could go for some one-on-one time with Jose Cuervo herself. She'd been called to Lay's office as soon as she came into work this morning, which she had expected after her saucy exit on Friday. She had not, however, expected Twitter to enter the mix. Her gut dropped; she had a horrible feeling she knew where this was going.

Mr. Lay reached for his cell phone and pressed a button. Before showing it to her, he added, "She did a search for my friends and added my coworkers too." He paused, and his beady eyes took on an excited gleam. "I must say your feed included quite a few interesting tidbits."

"Oh God." Verity didn't dare look at him. Her head sunk farther, her chin folding against her chest.

He cleared his throat, then read aloud: "If my boss tries to see my cooch one more damn time... hashtag eyes up front."

She closed her eyes. Her teeth sank into her bottom lip.

"Okay then." His voice grew quieter, but he read another one. "Hashtag replacing batteries in the rabbit."

This was humiliating. Her boss had not known how to use Twitter when she tweeted those. She knew that for a fact. She had checked when she got her account. If he'd been on there, she would've blocked him, but now the damage was done.

Her teeth bit harder into her lip. What did those texts have to do with why she was sitting here in his office? He was the one who should be feeling stupid, not her. Of course social cues were not really his forté...

He read a third tweet, his voice moving into a higher-pitched tone. "Hashtag pound Hudson. That bike messenger was named Hudson."

There it was.

This was all about Hudson. Just as she'd thought.

"I called the company where he works," Lay continued.

*Oh no.* Her head popped up, and she felt suddenly cold. Had she cost Hudson his job? He loved that job, and who knew if he could even get another one with all those tattoos. She didn't know a lot of bike messengers, but they all looked like they had criminal tendencies. Plus, they could move freely around the city, not sit behind a desk or enclosed in a cubicle from eight till five.

"What'd you do?" she asked.

His eyes narrowed for a split second, then he pushed his phone away and leaned back in his chair. He tugged at his collar. "Nothing." His finger began tapping at his desk. "But I did make it known that Mr. Hudson Fenn isn't to be bringing any more packages here."

That was it? He was still employed? Verity sat still, as if any movement might shake her boss's decision. Larold Lay was a loose cannon. Her eyes fell to the pen resting on his desk. It was the one he liked to throw on the floor and watch her bend over to get for him. Even thinking about it, her pulse picked up, and she started to get irritated about this whole thing. The level of douchebaggery was too high, and now he'd barred Hudson from bringing packages here? Her teeth ground against each other.

"… go there instead."

He'd been talking. She hadn't been listening. Oh, crap. She raised heated eyes to him, but cleared her throat too. She needed to go. She forced a calm and polite smile over her lips and asked, "What was that, Mr. Lay?"

He frowned slightly, looked nervous for a moment, and then shrugged. "Because I requested that Mr. Fenn not bring any more packages here, the company needs a day to add us to someone else's route. That means today they'll have a package there waiting to be brought over. I'd like for you to go get it, and hurry back. No hashtag pounding Hudson if you see him. Get my drift?"

She was stunned. "I have to go there?"

"Just today. And come back right away."

She jerked to her feet. She could go. No more sitting with Mr. Slimeball here. "Yes, Mr. Lay. That's quite fine with me." As she turned to go, she heard the small sound of something falling to the floor. She stopped, her back to him. She knew that sound. *No. Just no.*

"Uh, Verity?"

He sounded sweet, too sweet. Her teeth started grinding against each other again. She looked back, already knowing, and there it was. The damn pen was on the floor in front of his desk.

"Can you get that for me?" he asked, a gleam in his gaze. "You must've bumped it when you stood."

She knew damn well she hadn't. *Be professional, Verity! At least one of you should be.* "Uh…"

His phone rang, and she was granted a diversion. She kicked the pen under his desk. He frowned at her as he picked up the phone, then looked down from his side of the desk.

With her best fake smile plastered on her face, she lifted her shoulders. "Oops. My foot slipped," she whispered as she hurried out of there. Marge glanced up, startled by Verity's swift appearance, but Verity scurried through the door and was in Angie's office in record time.

"Do I even dare to ask what that was about?" Angie asked, looking up from her computer.

Verity's mouth pressed into a line. "My exit last Friday, before Hudson took me on that date."

Angie laid her arm over her forehead and struck a dramatic pose. "By the way, can I just say *swoon*? Took you to the Conservatory Garden and let you use his grandfather's Hasselblad? I mean, come on, that's the sweetest date ever."

"We *broke into* the Garden. We were trespassing."

"Even better." Angie pretended to fan herself. "I wouldn't have made it through the picnic before showing him my flowers." She winked. "Then and there, Verity. That's how I would've rolled with Mr. Tattoo-Rebel-Who's-All-Mysterious-About-MIT-Guy."

"Angie!" Verity hushed her before glancing over her shoulder. She'd confided the MIT suspicion over their second bottle of wine on Saturday when she went over to tell Angie about the date. Her friend was right, though. Friday had been like a dream. Then Saturday they'd exchanged texts and flirty tweets all day. But Sunday rolled around and… nothing. The wine hangover hadn't helped, but she'd convinced herself she'd be seeing him today.

Turns out, she probably would be, since she'd be going to his work. The fluttering in her stomach started again. She'd care later that he'd been banned from delivering packages to their office. Somehow, she'd get that corrected. She'd fix it. Mission: Bring Back Pussyfeathers was a go, but—she glanced at the clock—she needed to go pick up Larold's precious package first.

"What?" Angie asked, jarring Verity back to the present. "What's that look on your face?"

"I have to run an errand for Mr. Lay," Verity confessed. "He's barred Hudson from the office, so I have to go pick up a package."

Angie shook her head as Verity left.

Downstairs, Verity double-checked the name of the messenger company Hudson worked for, forwarded the office calls to her cell phone, and headed for the elevator. She took a cab to their headquarters—on Larold's tab this time—and felt a decidedly non-office-related feeling as she went through the glass double doors and walked toward the receptionist. This was just an office errand, but it was more. One person, one name made it so ridiculously different. *Hudson.*

She started to feel warm. This was ridiculous. Who was this guy to have this effect on her? A stolen cab. Breaking her into the Garden. Letting her use a family heirloom.

This was so dumb. She was lucky it hadn't gone horribly, horribly wrong.

What would her dad say if she called him from jail after Hudson's next big idea?

She was twenty-two. She was going places, putting together a real career and making her dad proud. Getting all hot and bothered over this guy, who she'd only known for a little while—no, *known* was too strong a word. She still knew nothing about his sketchy tattooed ass. She needed to get herself in check. Proceed with caution.

"Hello!" The receptionist smiled at her, pushing a button on the phone at the same time. "How can I help you?"

"Oh." She cleared her throat. This was business. "Verity Michaels. I'm here for SalesExportt.com. Mr. Lay has a package that needed to be picked up today."

"Yes." Recognition clicked in the receptionist's gaze, and she began looking around her desk. "You used to be on Hudson's route; isn't that right?"

"It is." Verity's smile felt etched into stone. Her cheeks were rock solid. "Actually, is he around right now?"

"Hudson?"

He worked here. It made sense the woman would know him, but did she have to sound so friendly about it? *Good grief, what do you care?* Evidently the conversation she'd had with herself wasn't sticking.

Then she heard the receptionist's voice double in cheer. "There he is! You're in luck. He's heading out." She pointed down the hall.

Verity looked.

She immediately wished she hadn't.

Her insides were sucked dry as she saw him. His blue eyes sparkled with laughter. His mouth was lifted in a smile. A girl walked with him. She said something, also laughing. Her cheeks were pink and her hand rested on his arm. He bent to hear what she was saying, but Verity's gaze fell to his hand, those tattooed fingers.

He was holding her hand.

**Verity Michaels** @VerityPics03
Fuck. That is all. #TheBoxesMustDie

**Verity Michaels** @VerityPics03
Hello, Vodka. We're going to be best friends again. #Kidding #VodkaIsMyBitch

**Verity Michaels** @VerityPics03
Hey, Mr. Lay and Mr. Lay's niece, guess who I'm blocking? #Fuuuuuck

## Chapter 9

### All the Fuckery in the World
### Helena Hunting

"Aren't you going to stop him?" the receptionist asked, her extra-smiley smile plastered all over her stupid face.

"He's busy. It can wait until the next time he delivers a package." Verity returned the smile, but it felt plastic and forced.

"I thought that's why you were here. He wasn't doing that any more? He's right there. I never miss a chance to get close to him." The receptionist giggled as she stood, smoothing her skirt over her tiny, prepubescent hips. She lifted one hand in the air, as if she were controlling traffic, or pumping her fist at some boy band concert.

Verity put her hands up in surrender fashion, hoping to dissuade the idiotic woman from bringing attention to either of them.

"Hudson!" the receptionist yelled.

Fortunately, the door had already closed behind them, making it impossible to hear her fingernails-on-chalkboard mating call.

Verity watched as he threw back his head in laughter at whatever the girl in the super-short sundress said. Then they disappeared around the corner.

"You can still catch him if you run," said the receptionist.

"I need to get back to work. Can I just sign for the package, please?" Verity tried to look less like a bitchy troll and more like the hot desk jockey she was supposed to be. Based on the receptionist's expression, she failed.

Verity collected her package, which was yet another bedazzled box, this time with flower-shaped jewels and zebra-print tape crisscrossed over and around the glitter paper covering the outside. It was like someone had tried to straightjacket the thing together.

Once outside, she scanned the street, hoping to find an ice cream shop to drown her sorrows in. She found an open bar and headed in there instead. She'd never done that before in her life, but when in Manhattan, do like the locals, right? Business drunk seemed pretty damn okay, even in the middle of the day. Thirty minutes and two shots later, plus a beer chaser, Verity was on her way back to work, the glitter-bombed package safe in her lap. She shook it, but as usual, it made no sound to indicate the weightless box actually contained anything.

Verity flipped it over in her hands, checking the corners for loose zebra tape, but the damn thing was sealed tight. Enraged by the stupid box, her stupid boss, and smooth-talking, two-timing Hudson, she hurled it on the floor of the cab. What she really wanted was to pretend it was Hudson's balls and puncture the cardboard with her pointy heel. Instead, she picked it up and inspected the damage. One corner was dented, and picking at the spot, she used her nail to create a tiny hole.

With skills gathered from binge-watching *CSI*, Verity used the flashlight feature on her phone, nearly blinding herself in her quest to uncover the contents. Holding her phone to the hole, she attempted to get a peek inside, but all she could see was darkness and glitter.

Then the cab stopped in front of her building, ending her mission to reveal the mysterious contents. She threw money at the driver and stumbled out of the cab, narrowly missing a sewer grate. Recovering herself, Verity beelined inside and straight for the bathroom, the drinks having worked their way through her system. Verity set the package on the floor, hoping someone else's pee particles would contaminate it. Her hands were covered in sparkles. She used a piece of toilet paper to pick the box back up to avoid direct contact. No matter how much soap she used to wash her hands, she couldn't seem to get sparkle free. Glitter was the herpes of crafting.

Two minutes later she was back in the elevator, heading up to Mr. Lay's office with the package tucked under her arm. She hated him for making her pick up the damn thing. Not only was her outfit now covered in glitter, her Hudson fantasies were tainted by the pretty little blonde with her hand on his tattooed arm and their fingers laced together.

Verity wanted *her* plain hand twined with his decorated one. Or she had until today. That would have made an awesome picture. She could envision it in a frame. The elevator dinged. She took a deep breath, preparing for the day's second interaction with Mr. Lay.

Marge said nothing, didn't even look up as Verity pushed through the doors to Mr. Lay's office, where she found him with a pair of tweezers up his nose. He dropped them in a hurry, shoving them under a pile of papers.

"Ms. Michaels. You're back?"

Verity really wanted to say *no*, but somewhere inside her, professionalism fought its way through her day-drinking buzz and Hudson-related anger. She kept her mouth shut as she crossed his office, lifted her arm, and dropped the box on the desk like she was shitting it out of her armpit.

He huffed his displeasure. Snatching it up, he leaned back in his chair, crossing one leg over the other. The position hiked his pants up, creating a moose knuckle at his crotch. Oblivious to his ballsy display, Mr. Lay inspected the dented corner, poking his finger in the tiny hole. "What happened to my package?"

Verity's eyes lifted from the highlighted package in his lap to the one he was holding. She leaned on his desk and pretended to examine it as well.

When she returned her gaze to Mr. Lay, she found him staring not at the slightly mangled box, but at her cleavage. Verity straightened immediately. "I have no idea. That's how it was when I picked it up."

"You didn't do this, Ms. Michaels?"

Verity crossed her arms over her chest in mock shock. "Of course not!"

"This is unacceptable." Mr. Lay picked up the phone, punched viciously at the buttons, and gestured to the chair opposite his desk. "Have a seat."

"But—"

"I can't have my package tossed around like this." He gestured to the glittery monstrosity.

"I may have dropped it in the cab," she mumbled into her

shoulder.

Mr. Lay put his hand over the receiver. "You may have dropped it?"

"Okay. I did drop it. I don't see what the big deal is. Gravity is a thing." She thought better of her tone and added, "Sir."

Mr. Lay replaced the receiver and put his hands in his armpits. "Dropping my package scares me. I need what's in here. A lot. So much. Very."

Verity looked at her feet while he pontificated about his package and his needs. Business drunk wanted to laugh. "It doesn't make a sound and weighs nothing, so if there is something in there, it has to be pretty damn light, or small, or taped to the inside so it doesn't move around."

He raised his eyebrows, seeming to search for a response.

"What I mean is, your package is well protected," Verity added quickly. Damn it. Her alcohol-induced verbal vomit was going to get her fired.

"You really want to know what's in my package, don't you?"

She ignored his double entendre. "Of course I do! Who wouldn't? You made me traipse halfway across the city to pick this one up because you didn't want to wait until tomorrow. What the hell is in there? Is it porn? Used women's underpants?" *Jesus.* She really needed to muzzle herself.

Mr. Lay leaned back in his chair and uncrossed his legs. His pants remained hiked up, still strangling his package. Verity tried not to let her eyes drop. It was difficult. It appeared as though Mr. Lay was packing some serious heat under there—unless he'd stuck a sock in to beef it up. She wouldn't put it past him.

"Come out for a drink after work, and I'll tell you what's in the box," he said, trying for nonchalant.

"Seriously?" Verity stopped considering the size of his package and focused on the package on his desk.

"Seriously."

"You're paying." Verity wished she wasn't three drinks to the wind, otherwise those words would never have come out of her mouth.

His grin was somewhere between pompous and psychotic. She already regretted her agreement. "I wouldn't have it any other way."

He was such a weirdo. She stared at him for a few seconds. "I need to get back to work. I've been away from the desk all day."

"Of course, Ms. Michaels."

She left to the sound of a pen hitting the floor.

**Verity Michaels** @VerityPics03
I'm not looking at your package. I think it is dead anyway. #DeadInside #YouKilledIt

**Verity Michaels** @VerityPics03
Okay I tossed your package. Not your salad. Settle down. #MoreBusinessDrinkPlease

**Verity Michaels** @VerityPics03
Going to drinks with Lay sounds great. Super great. How come he's not always covered in glitter? #LifeMystery #DrinkingAnswersQuestions

# Chapter 10

## Package Inspectoritis
## Helena Hunting

It took about an hour for her buzz to wear off, giving her the rest of the afternoon to stew over Hudson and the pretty blonde, as well as the contents of Mr. Lay's sparkly box. No way in hell was she going out alone with him.

She zipped back upstairs to corner Angie at her desk. "Um, hey! We're going with Larold for drinks after work."

"Oh, wow. Tempting, but I can't. I have a date."

"What? Come on. I need you!"

"Joseph sent flowers while you were on your road trip."

"That's all it takes for you to bail on a friend?" Verity asked, half teasing, half panicked.

Angie shrugged. "Yours is such a tempting offer. Joseph's thinking of getting a tattoo, and he wants to discuss it. Speaking of that sort of thing, how'd the package pick-up go? Did you run into Hudson? Did you find an empty storage closet to molest him in? Why do you have glitter on your face?"

That was too many questions. "What time is your date? Can't you come for a quick drink?"

Angie crossed her endless, flawless legs. "What's going on?"

"I agreed to go out with Mr. Lay after work. I need you to come with me so I'm not alone."

"Why would you do that?"

"I was drunk, and he said he'd tell me what was in the packages if I went."

"And you believe him?" Angie looked at her like she'd lost her mind, which very well might be the case. "Wait a second, did you say you were drunk? At work? Did you go out for drinks with Hudson? Did you have sex in a dirty bathroom stall? Does he have a gigantic dick?"

"None of those things happened." Although she'd actually fantasized that exact scenario. "I saw him with another woman. They were holding hands."

The smile slipped off Angie's face. "Oh, Verity. I'm so sorry. He was so badass. And hot. That really sucks."

"Whatever. It's not like he was my boyfriend or anything. And he probably has an extensive criminal record, considering his propensity for theft and B and E. If anything, it's saved me from being an accomplice and ending up in prison, selling phallic vegetables for contraband cigarettes."

"You really have some weird fears about prison." Angie shook her head. "He was so hot. I'll message Joseph and move the time back from seven to eight."

"Oh, you're a lifesaver."

Angie patted her hand and gave her a piteous smile, then pulled out her phone to speed text her date.

Verity returned to her desk, where she flipped back and forth between spreadsheets and Pinterest pictures of hot guys with tattoos. At five-oh-five, the elevator doors dinged and Mr. Lay stepped out. His suit was buttoned and he'd clearly spent some time in the restroom managing his hair. It was slicked back, making him look like a modern-day gangster. He did absolutely nothing for her girl parts.

Verity shot Angie a text as he strode over to her desk.

"Ready to go, Ms. Michaels?"

She gave him a fake smile. "Almost, Mr. Lay. I just need to save this spreadsheet."

He sat on the edge of her desk and pretended to line up her pens while staring at her cleavage.

Her phone buzzed on her desk with a new text. Verity nabbed it and shoved it in her purse as Angie came strutting out of the elevator like it was her own personal runway.

"Ready to go?" she asked brightly.

Mr. Lay looked confused.

"I invited Angie along," Verity said. "I hope you don't mind. I wouldn't want anyone to get the wrong idea, right?"

"Of course not. Angie, you know you're always welcome to join," Mr. Lay said to her breasts.

The three of them left the building together and walked down the street to a bar. It seemed to have a bit of a nautical theme. Verity had never been inside before, as she usually preferred to get much farther from the office than this before slowing down. She ordered the most expensive martini and made it a double. Her phone buzzed in her purse again, and she hid it under the table to check. Her stomach did an annoying flip when she saw there were three messages from Hudson.

Felony Ever After

> They changed my route today. I missed seeing you.

Verity scoffed. Smooth-talking bastard. The second and third messages made her furious:

> What are you up to tonight?

> I have pictures for you.

Friday night she'd had her tongue in his mouth, and less than six hours ago she'd seen him with another woman. She wondered if the blonde knew she was being played. She put her phone away and focused on Mr. Lay, who was talking about himself. This made it easy to polish off her martini and order another. Her phone buzzed again, half an hour later.

> Honeybee? Are you ignoring me?

Annoyed at the nickname, Verity finally responded. Her answer was simple:

> **Yes.**

His reply was almost immediate.

> **You do realize you've responded, so you're not ignoring me any more, right?**

Verity refused to reply to that one.
A few minutes later, another message came through.

> **Where are you?**

This time Verity gave in, determined to shut him up as she typed in the words and pressed send:

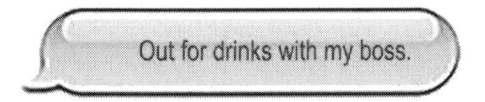

> **Out for drinks with my boss.**

She waited for some kind of angry response, but none came. The last time he'd asked where she was he'd showed up at the bar. She looked around, expecting him to appear. He didn't.

A few minutes later, Angie excused herself to the bathroom. It was already seven-fifteen. If she didn't leave soon, she'd miss her date with Joseph. Verity still didn't want to be alone with Larold, his perfect teeth, or his awkward advances.

"I should probably be heading home."

Mr. Lay put his hand over hers. "I thought you wanted to talk about my package."

Verity clamped her lips together. She had a better idea than she wanted about what was going on in his pants after today. A flash of light outside caught her attention, and she glanced toward the wall of windows. Standing on the street, a beanie pulled low on his head, was Hudson. In one hand was an envelope. In the other was his phone. Her own buzzed in her purse.

She turned her attention back to Mr. Lay and panicked a little, hurt and anger crowding out any good sense she had left. Leaning in close, she used her best smutty porn-star voice, "I think I like the mystery better."

When she glanced back to the windows lining the front of the bar, Hudson was gone. Heavy disappointment settled in her gut. She'd never been much of a game player, and the vindication didn't feel nearly as good as she wanted it to. Plus she'd ruined her chance to find out what was in the damn packages.

Angie returned from the bathroom and announced she had to go, giving Verity the perfect excuse to leave as well. Mr. Lay looked unhappy, which was the highlight of Verity's night so far. She and Angie left for the subway, leaving Larold with the bill.

Verity checked her phone on the train. She only had one message. It was from Hudson:

> Not cool.

Verity typed a quick response and pressed send before she lost her nerve:

> Now you know how it feels.

He replied right away.

> ????

Verity punched at the digital keyboard and had to try three times before she got her angry reply right. She was a terrible semi-drunk typer:

> I saw you with your other girlfriend.

He responded quickly:

> OTHER girlfriend?

It made her rage that she had to spell it out for him.

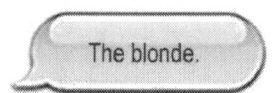

> The blonde.

On the walk to her building from her stop, she stumbled on a grate that caught her heel, which broke off as her ankle twisted uncomfortably. None of the people passing by stopped or even looked up to see if she was okay. It made her miss her friendly Florida town where at least three people would have made sure she wasn't injured. Instead, she hobbled to the front door of her apartment building, feeling extra sorry for herself.

Hudson didn't reply between the time she got into the elevator and limped to her apartment door. She shoved the key in the lock and practically fell inside. She slapped the wall in search of the light switch and screamed as she spotted a figure sitting on her couch in the semi-darkness.

She whipped her broken heel in his direction—she assumed it was a man based on the jeans and black hoodie. It sailed past his head and hit the wall across the room. She took a moment to be impressed with herself before she followed with her purse, which he caught before it could hit him in the face.

"I'm calling the police," she yelled, wondering why he looked so familiar and why he hadn't left her apartment the second she opened the door.

"Whoa, settle down." Hudson pushed his hood down with a tattooed hand.

"You broke into my apartment? How the hell did you get in here?" Verity's limbs felt weak and wobbly. Her heart thundered in her ears. Adrenaline coursed through her veins and tingles set up shop between her legs. Goddamnit. Why did he have to be so hot?

He raised an eyebrow. "I climbed the fire escape. You left your window wide open. Anyone could get in here."

"Get out!" Verity pointed to the door. "How did you know

this was my place?"

"Bike messengers have ways." Hudson tossed a large envelope on the coffee table. "I just wanted to drop off the pictures from Friday."

"You could have slipped them under the door instead of coming into my apartment."

"I couldn't get in the building," he said calmly. "I also thought I'd get some clarification on a couple of things."

"Leave!" Verity pointed to the door, but she wasn't very convincing in her assertiveness—even to herself. Her knees finally gave out, and she melted to the floor.

Hudson pushed to his feet and crossed to where she'd crumpled dramatically. For a few seconds she was at eye level with his crotch. Then he crouched down and settled his elbows on his knees. The silver ball in his mouth popped out between his lips and slid back and forth once before it disappeared back inside. His blue eyes locked onto hers.

"Are you drunk?"

She sat up straighter and pushed her chest out until the buttons on her blouse strained. "I'm buzzed."

"Why were you out for drinks with your boss? You hate him."

"Because I want to know what's in those damn packages, and because when I picked up one from your main office today, I saw you all cozied up to that cute little blonde." Martinis were the worst kind of truth serum for Verity.

"You mean my *other* girlfriend?" The right side of Hudson's mouth quirked up.

"You're an asshole."

"You should probably know, that cute little blonde is one of my half-sisters, and she's thirteen. I was taking her out for lunch."

Verity's mouth opened to fire a snarky response, but the only thing that came was a quiet, cracked, "Oh." The girl's age would explain her questionable fashion choices.

"So back to clarifying..." Hudson cleared his throat. "If she's my *other* girlfriend, what are you?"

*Oh shit.* It was a trap. She'd baited it herself. Verity folded her legs under her and pushed up, forgetting about the ankle she'd rolled. She yelped and fell forward, face-planting into Hudson's chest and knocking them both off balance. He landed on his ass, and she landed on top of him. It would have been the perfect position under different circumstances.

She blew her hair out of her face and struggled to get up. "I'm just the girl you're stalking."

Hudson wrapped an arm around her waist, keeping her where she was. "I think you like me stalking you."

Verity snorted a very unfeminine snort. "Well, you're clearly a criminal, so of course you'd think that."

"We're back to that, are we? Don't you think the stereotype is getting a little old?" The arm around her waist tightened. His eyes dropped from hers and focused on her chest pressed against his. "I don't know if you know this, but this shirt is pretty much transparent. I can see your bra through it. And that's a lot of cleavage you've got going on there." He stuck a finger in it to demonstrate. "If I was your boyfriend, I don't think I'd be all that happy that you wore it to work today. Especially paired with this skirt and knowing what a weirdo your boss is." Hudson's hand eased lower to her ass. He gave it a little squeeze.

"I guess it's a good thing you're not my boyfriend then, isn't it?"

"Definitely a good thing." Hudson squeezed harder and shifted under her. "Way better that I'm just stalking your fine ass."

They stared at each other for a half-second before Verity yanked off his beanie, shoved her hands into his hat-head hair and plastered her mouth to his.

Hudson cupped the back of her head and rolled them over so he was on top. The seam at the back of Verity's skirt gave way with a huge tear as she opened her legs so Hudson could fit himself between them. They dry-humped the living hell out of each other as they made out in the middle of her living room floor.

Verity grabbed the hem of his hoodie and yanked it up, pulling it over his head when there was a break in the kiss. His white T-shirt came with it. Under all those clothes was a seriously cut body covered in ink. She'd expected as much. It wouldn't make a whole lot of sense to have hand and neck tattoos if the rest of the merchandise wasn't going to be decorated the same way.

Verity ran her hands over his chest and down his abs.

"Badass enough for a stalker?" Hudson asked, that damn dimply smirk curving the corner of his mouth.

"You must be the king of badass stalkers." Verity tried to pull him back down for another kiss—she was really starting to dig that tongue piercing—but Hudson sat back on his heels.

He untucked her shirt from her skirt. "I don't think you'll be wearing this shirt to work again."

"Why not?"

"It doesn't have any buttons." He grabbed the hem on either

side and pulled. The buttons popped off, pinging against his ripped chest—seriously, all that biking did a body good. She didn't even care that he'd ruined her sort-of slutty work shirt.

Verity thanked the gods of bra design for the little heart-shaped front clasp on the one she was wearing. She opened it and set the girls free. They were like homing devices for Hudson's hands. He cupped them immediately, separating his fingers so her nipples peeked through.

*Jesus.* He really did look like a criminal with all that ink—an incredibly hot criminal who'd broken into her house to bring her pictures taken with an heirloom camera during an illicit visit to the Conservatory Garden. He even had a few scars littered across his chest and one on his arm to complete the criminal look. She wondered if there was a bullet wound scar somewhere.

Hudson ducked his head and sucked one of her happy nipples into his mouth. Verity moaned and arched as she fumbled around, searching for the buckle on his belt. Finding it, she freed the clasp and went for the button on his jeans. There wasn't a zipper to make him easier to access. It was buttons all the way down. It was hard to concentrate while he continued the nipple sucking, but she finally managed to get them all undone.

Verity took a deep breath. This was the moment of truth. She shoved her hand down his pants, praying she'd find something in there to match the rest of his hotness. He was commando, because of course—badass criminals don't do underwear.

She wrapped her fingers around his shaft. "Thank God," she muttered when her thumb and forefinger didn't touch. Not even close, actually. Verity had small hands; if her fingers touched, it meant unfortunate things.

Hudson lifted his head. "Worried I wasn't going to have a

dick?"

Verity stroked the length, getting a feel for how much there was, until she hit something that didn't feel like it belonged. She looked between them, but it was dark down there. She put a hand on his chest so she could check it out a little better.

"Is that a—" She brushed the steel with her thumb. Not only was Hudson sporting an above-average cock, it was pierced. Thankfully it wasn't tattooed. That would cross the badass line into really weird. Larold territory. She met Hudson's amused gaze. "I want to know what that feels like."

"Go ahead and touch it all you want." Hudson's mouth went slack as she stroked him a few times.

"No." Verity licked her lips. "I mean I want to know what it feels like from the inside."

Hudson grinned. "Should I assume you're not talking about the inside of your mouth?"

Verity thought for less than a second. She could do the whole blow job thing another time. Besides, knowing her luck, she'd end up sucking the ball right off the piercing and that would result in a trip to the hospital—a place she was only slightly more interested in visiting than jail.

She'd been fantasizing about being pounded by Hudson since he'd stolen the cab and dropped her off at this very apartment. She shook her head. "Not the inside of my mouth."

"Just to clarify, are you asking me to fuck you?"

"Yes, please."

Hudson pulled his wallet from the back pocket of his jeans and slapped it on the coffee table beside them. Then he stripped off his pants. He also had ink on his very muscular legs. Verity would check that out later. After the sex. Hudson didn't bother taking off her skirt. He just shoved it up to her hips and dragged her panties down her legs.

He lifted his hot gaze to hers. "Did you bedazzle your pussy for me?"

"What?"

"It's all sparkly."

Verity lifted her head and tried to see what Hudson was seeing, but she'd have to pull off a seriously difficult yoga pose to make that happen.

He rubbed the crest of her pelvis with his thumb and held it up for her to see: pink sparkles.

"Mr. Lay's stupid package was wrapped in sparkle paper today. It's probably everywhere."

Hudson nodded like he understood. He dropped his eyes again, along with his hand. He rubbed a slow circle around her clit, then went lower, sliding a finger inside. "Later, I'm going to eat that pretty little pussy of yours. It's absolutely perfect."

Verity was sure all her sex parts had just exploded in their own glitter bomb of excitement. "That sounds like a lot of fun."

"Oh, it will be." Hudson's tongue piercing popped out as he flipped his wallet open, retrieved a condom, ripped it from the package, and rolled it on. He grabbed Verity by the hips and dragged her closer. "Wrap your legs around my waist."

A shiver raced up her spine, goosebumps breaking out across her skin. Hudson circled her clit with the head of his cock, then slid low, teasing her with the tip.

"How do you want it, Honeybee?"

"Huh?" Verity was too focused on the feel of his cock nudging her to get the question.

"How do you want me to fuck you?" He leaned over her,

slipped low, and eased inside. "Hard and fast, or slow and easy?"

His question inspired an image of being pretzeled into some porn-star position and pounded. It was exactly what she expected. Except that wasn't what she got.

Hudson stayed deep, rolling his hips, hitting sensitive places inside her body. Verity held on to his shoulders, submerged in sensation as that piercing worked its magic and brought her to the edge of an orgasm, then dropped-kicked her right over the edge into heaven.

Hudson cradled the back of her head in his hand so it wouldn't bang on the floor with every thrust. "Next time," he said against her lips.

"Next time, what?"

"Next time hard and fast so you can use your favorite hashtag."

**Verity Michaels** @VerityPics03
Tight pants aren't work appropriate. #MooseKnuckle #TheStruggleIsReal

**Verity Michaels** @VerityPics03
Sometimes the fantasy is better than reality. Not in this case. #PoundHudson #SmoothCriminal #Braggy #BigDick

**Verity Michaels** @VerityPics03
What the hell is in the box? #CraftHerpes

# Chapter 11

## Breakfast of Champions
## Nina Bocci

Sometime in the middle of the night, a police siren's *bloop* woke a very sated Verity out of a very dead sleep. Shivering, she turned into Hudson's arms, seeking warmth. The chill from the night air danced across her naked skin, lining it with goosebumps. *We need a blanket*, she thought but then changed her mind.

The bright yellow streetlight shone through the apartment windows and across the ink on Hudson's chest. He looked like an unfinished coloring book. Just for her. Some areas were only outlined in black. Others were blasts of bold color that melted into his skin. Lightly, she traced the thick and thin lines. The swirls and waves ran like multicolored veins up his arms, down his ribcage before disappearing beneath… nothing.

He slept in the nude, like any self-respecting, master-tattooed criminal thief would.

Smiling to herself, she turned her attention to his face. Over his strong jaw and scruffy cheeks, his eyes remained shut, his breathing deep and rhythmic.

Verity would never have ever imagined herself in bed with a guy like this. Her father was big on respectable appearances, and maybe that had rubbed off on her. Maybe judgey-ness was inherited. But thank God something had pulled her past that—sheer hotness, maybe. She giggled softly.

He was so different than her first impression. So different than anyone she'd ever known. And actually, maybe she was also a little different since their first meeting. She wanted to be. Much of him was still unknown to her—although quite a bit less than a few hours ago—but his easy confidence and kindness were contagious. She could feel them seeping into her, warming her, even if they weren't natural to her yet.

She shifted to get a better look at him. He'd stolen a taxi to get her home safe. Just yesterday she'd read online about a woman being carjacked not far away. Hudson had been right to worry that the cabbie-vs-road rager argument might be dangerous.

His dick piercing winked in the window light, cutting through the darkness and her thoughts. She winked back, giddy upon remembering his words. *"Should I assume you're not talking about the inside of your mouth?"*

The plan seized her from the inside out. Bold she was not. Ever, really. But with Hudson, something spurred her on. Maybe it was his reckless abandon of convention or the way he pushed her to be free. She felt it warming her again.

She wanted to borrow some of his bold. Maybe inherit it a little. With him, she might find out who Verity really was.

"Midnight snack," she whispered and slipped from beneath his arm.

As she moved, he remained asleep, but his brows worried together. His mouth slanted and his arm stretched, as if seeking her out. Her heart squeezed and her stomach dipped. His long, lean body shifted, scratching against the carpet as he slung an arm over his eyes. The other scratched his stomach before falling to rest against her leg.

Their clothes were strewn across her living room. Belts, shoes, jeans, and then she spied his T-shirt. She pulled it over her head, relishing the scent that surrounded her. Looking down at herself in it, Verity realized she looked wanton—all mussed and ruffled, the picture of properly fucked.

She needed to get this show on the road.

Tucking her hair behind her ear, she sized up her approach. She wanted nothing more than to feast on him, savor him fully and feel the ball at his tip against her lips. His hands in her hair. Her name on his breath. But she needed to move slowly, gently, for maximum effect.

Careful not to disturb him, she moved into position from the side. The prickly rug rubbed against her belly. It wasn't helping the butterflies already in there. Deep breaths in and out were her saving grace as she inched her mouth down and around him. Once, twice, three times, and then she was no lady.

Lust roared through her on a moan and took over. All sense of slow and steady went out the window on the breeze. In a flash, he was awake.

"Verity," he gasped, muscles bunching beneath her hand as she dipped again. "Verity, what're—oh, fuck."

She nipped at him playfully. Just a bit, but it was enough for Hudson's entire body to snap with tension.

"Midnight snack," she informed him, dizzy with need as she plunged her mouth around his cock again. One hand cupped him, and she reached the other between her legs to lessen the throbbing.

Hudson caught her hand before it hit home. "No," he ground out, his body angling up off of the rug.

She knew he must be getting close. When she tried to reach her pussy again, he slapped her hand away.

"My turn," he demanded, smoothing his palm over her ass and down her thigh.

With each pass he got closer to where she wanted him. Needed him. Two fingers traced from her hip to her thigh and back up. He swirled them around until finally, she couldn't take it anymore.

"Please," she begged around his cock, rubbing the tip between her lips. She shook her ass in jest. Something to spur him into action.

"Oh, Country Girl, you don't know what you're in for."

He surged up and slid backward to lean against the couch cushions they'd pulled down last night. His hard cock slipped out of her mouth, and she whimpered, a full-blown you-took-away-my-candy whimper. She was fairly certain she pouted as well.

"Give it here," he said with a light slap to her ass.

Instead she crawled away, brushing her knees against the

rug, taking her ass out of his grasp as she looked over her shoulder.

He'd slouched comfortably, like he was ready to relax and watch television, but it just so happened he was naked. His eyes, though. They let her know this was no game to him. He was going to devour her.

Oh, how she wished he would. With narrowed eyes, she wiggled her ass for him to come to her.

"I said," he repeated slowly, his finger signaling for her to come forward, "give it here."

"No," she quipped, marching away on all fours.

Quickly, he caught her ankle and pulled her back. The rug burn would hurt like hell in the morning, but for now, it did nothing but kindle the fire. His legs were spread, his cock jutted up, and she tried to reach for it …

"Not yet," he barked, pulling one of her legs over his body so she straddled him, still facing away. "Give it here," he urged, laying his hands on her calves. He massaged, deep and just a tad too hard, and waited for her to catch on to what he wanted.

"You can't mean…" She dropped her head to look at him from below. Upside down, he peered at her, watching her breasts sway with her shuddering breath.

"I can mean," he said, smacking his lips as his eyes drank in her pussy. "And I want." His hands came to rest below her hips, guiding her back slowly. Anticipation choked her as her pussy came close enough to feel his warm breath.

Shifting, he tipped her hips up to meet his waiting mouth. His tongue dipped and swirled like the ink across his arms. Slowly, he kissed her. Fucked her with his mouth until her arms, weak like jelly, gave out. She managed to prop herself up at an angle: ass in the air, her forearms on his legs.

"You had your midnight snack," he said against her pussy. "This is my breakfast."

Verity pushed back as Hudson lunged forward, burying his tongue inside her. He ravaged her, unrelenting, unforgiving.

"Holy fu—" she began when she felt the ball, the tiny silver ball wreaking havoc on her clit.

His hands came up and slid her apart. Fingers, tongue, lips, and a little teeth. She was melting from the inside out.

"Please," she gasped, reaching for something to hold on to before she fell.

He wouldn't let her slip. Not yet. Not until he'd had his fill. She knew that even in the haze of her building orgasm. She felt him shift, legs spreading while his upper body shifted to take the weight of her legs onto his shoulders.

Closer to his mouth.

Jesus Christ.

She surrounded him, and he her.

Her cheek brushed his cock, and he moaned, the vibration rumbling through her entire being.

"You fucked..." She paused, her eyes rolling back, her awareness heightened from the sensations of his lips on hers. "You took. Now I want."

With a cry, she took him in her mouth again and lavished, meeting his actions with her own. For every lick, suck, and nibble, she gave a swallow, a pump, and a run along the shaft with her teeth, which she'd realized he loved.

"Verity." A warning. He was going to come.

"Hudson." An answer. She wasn't stopping.

She was lost in the single-minded focus of making him come, of losing herself to his mouth and—fuck! He added fingers now.

"Come on me," he begged.

He was losing it. They both felt it. Precise movements gave way to harried and frantic actions, that final climb to the top before they both fell over.

One more time she swallowed, deep, and with a groan he let go. She kept going, enjoying the way all her senses lit up on the build of her own orgasm.

"Please, Verity," she heard him say. Or she thought she did. She teetered on the wire until he pinched the nerve, and she snapped.

Overwhelmed by the emotional surge, Verity felt tears streaming down her face, running over her nipples and dropping on his still-shaking legs.

He slowed, kissing her reverently before helping her weak body into a more comfortable position.

Quietly, they laid together, breathing heavily. Verity felt dizzy, weak, and happier than she'd been in forever. After a few minutes, Hudson's breathing slowed to a normal pace. She figured he had typical-man syndrome and had fallen back asleep like a lump after he'd destroyed her.

"That was…" he began, surprising her. He tucked her in beside him so they laid facing each other. He reached up to smooth away her lingering tears. "No words, Honeybee," he said, brushing another tear from the top of her breast.

She had words, but she didn't use them.

He broke the silence eventually. "I'm feeling very awake," he announced. "So tell me, what are your receptionist dreams?"

Verity laughed. "Receptionist dreams? What do you mean?"

"Well, is that what you want to be when you grow up? Most Southerners I've met in the city have a dream they're willing to die trying for: sing on Broadway, trade on Wall Street, something..." He pushed her hair off her forehead and kissed it.

"I guess I'm different than those people. Please tell me they're not all past girlfriends?" Verity gave him a glare.

"I like when you're possessive." He touched the end of her nose.

"I came here because my dream fell through. I opened a photography business in Florida—I even had business cards—but the demand wasn't there. Or I wasn't good enough. Whatever." She looked away toward the window for a moment.

"I'm sure you were good enough. You've got a great eye." He squeezed her hand and smiled at her, but she could just see it in profile.

"Thanks. I really thought I could do it. But it didn't work out. So this is my fall back: being a real adult. My dad had a connection that got me the job. He prides himself on being a businessman. The corporate world is what's real to him." She shook her head.

"Oh, papa can't do you like that. Not cool at all." Hudson

*tsk*ed at her. "You can be whatever you want." He made a buzzing noise against the top of her head.

"Tell me about you," she said, wishing it were as simple as he made it seem. "How'd you decide you wanted to be covered in tattoos and riding a bike?" She traced his chest with her fingertip.

"I like colors. Listen, can I grab a shower? Do you mind?" Hudson shifted and pulled his arm from underneath her.

"Sure." She was too orgasm-floppy to fight him. Had she said something wrong?

She waited for what felt like forever, but as her endorphins faded, so did her wakefulness, and she drifted off.

**Verity Michaels** @VerityPics03
#69

**Verity Michaels** @VerityPics03
#69

**Verity Michaels** @VerityPics03
#69

# Chapter 12

## Midnight Snack
### Nina Bocci

Another *bloop-bloop* woke Verity a few hours later. This time it was her coffee pot. It filled her small apartment with the scent of a much-needed caffeine boost.

Naked save for Hudson's T-shirt, she sat up, stretching and relishing her sore muscles. His clothes were gone: shoes no longer flung near the door, hoodie missing.

She didn't let herself frown on the outside, but she couldn't control the sadness that spread from within.

"Oh good, you're up," Hudson said cheerily from the kitchen.

Relief flooded her body until her smile split open across her face. "You stayed," she breathed, standing up quickly and catching a hold of the couch.

"I've made breakfast," he said lazily, seeming distracted by her nipples, which had perked up in the morning air. His eyes blazed over them, drinking them in. His coffee sat forgotten on her small counter.

"Hungry?" she asked, stretching so his shirt rode up over her belly.

He nodded. "I—food," he managed, hitching his thumb over his shoulder.

She sashayed around the arm of the couch—a move Angie would have been proud of, had she seen it. "Good morning."

Up on her toes, she kissed him sweetly on both cheeks and then his lips. Her hand rested on his waist and toyed with the skin there, covered only loosely by his hoodie.

"Eat?"

She'd reduced him to caveman. How fabulous.

"Mmmm," she murmured. "That looks amazing. What did you make?"

She peeked over his shoulder to see bowls of fruit and yogurt and orange juice set up.

He wasn't listening. She knew this because his eyes were glazed over and still staring at her nipples through his shirt. Mr. Lay did it all the time, and it was creepy. But this was empowering—and new. She'd converted Hudson to his baser form simply by wearing a shirt—plain, white, innocuous. Who needed pricey, fancy lingerie? She was going to Hanes.

"I always do yoga in the morning before breakfast. Do you mind?" she said, suddenly both bold and a liar. He *was* rubbing off on her...

He shook his head.

Verity sat on the arm of the couch, making sure she was properly covered. Glancing over her shoulder, she fought to keep a straight face. He stared—transfixed and hard. Nothing was a secret in those well-worn jeans.

Reaching up, she lifted her arms high over her head, flexing and stretching as his shirt rode up to her waist. She heard him swallow. She purred, or at least she tried. She drew on every trick she'd seen Angie pull. Every arch of her back or thrust of her chest was meant to drive him insane.

And insane he was.

Hudson practically vibrated, his hands clenched into fists and his chest heaving.

"It's this new couch yoga," Verity ad libbed, enjoying the power she felt surging through her. She linked her arms over her head and slowly leaned back, using every abdominal muscle she could muster to balance until her shoulders were on the couch. Her butt remained on the arm.

Hudson launched into action. In the amount of time it took her to blink, he moved from behind the couch to loom over her like a menace. "What was your hashtag?" he asked as he pulled off his hoodie.

She'd been amazed by all of the ink in the darkness last night, but she was struck dumb seeing it in the light of day.

"Hmm? Cat got your tongue?" With slow precision, Hudson plucked open the buttons on his jeans, laughing when she gasped at his cock springing free. Before his pants fell to the ground, he popped a condom out of his pocket and set it on her stomach.

It may as well have been made of fire the way it burned her.

"Was it strike Hudson? No, no," he teased, easing open

her legs as they dangled over the arm of the couch. "Or pummel Hudson? No, no, that's not it either." With his thumbs he massaged his way up her thighs. "I wish I could remember." He tore the condom open and rolled it down his cock, his eyes never leaving hers.

Verity couldn't form the words. *Pound Hudson* danced in her mind. The words bubbled in her throat. They pooled in her mouth but stayed there while he lined himself up to take her.

He wrapped his hand around himself, stroking. The tip, and that damnable piercing, rubbed against her clit. Slowly, he slid his cock up, made a circle around her nerves, and then down again. A dip, then a repeat. She felt it all. His fingers swooped over the head and stroked downward to his base. Everything brushed against her.

He grunted, eyes rolling back. He was losing himself in the sensation. "Th-thump?" he offered, shakily.

Verity shifted her weight, and as her body lifted, he sunk into her. They both sighed, eyes screwed shut, mouths open.

"Pound," she finally managed, putting her hands over his at her waist.

Hudson was like a rubber band pulled too tightly. He snapped, reared back, and thrust.

She was done for.

She heard a chuckle, dark and haunting. "Pound Hudson. That's right." He drove into her hard, fast, and as unrelenting as his tongue had been last night.

The threadbare arm of the couch singed her back, her ass, everywhere that made contact as he, quite literally, pounded into her.

Sweat formed at his brow. His muscles bunched, corded, and rolled with the effort of keeping up the pace. He gripped her ass, fingers digging in.

Verity wanted more, needed more to lose herself in it all. She reached up, holding her breasts in her palms. The shirt scratched wonderfully against her nipples. She opened her eyes and smiled up at him.

"Show me," he pleaded, his tongue reaching out to moisten his lips. "Please."

A second of shyness shrouded her before she pushed through and pinched and pulled at her nipples.

His pace faltered. "Fuck."

"More?" She grinned devilishly when he nodded, eyes hooded and trained on her tits.

She lifted the hem of the shirt to reveal her breasts, one and then the other. "They're lonely," Verity said.

"Ungh." Hudson surveyed the scene for a moment and said, "Back up. I want them too."

"Greedy," she said, frowning when he slipped from her.

He kicked off his jeans as she crab-crawled back to lay fully on the cushions. His long, lithe body covered hers, and he kissed her, nipping her bottom lip. He trailed a line of kisses from her lips, down her throat, until he reached her breasts. He pushed them together to run his tongue across the tips, around each breast, and through the valley between them. He left no inch untouched.

She shivered as the cool air met the wetness from his lips. She was heated and chilled at the same time, and it was glorious.

His nose ran along her jaw to her ear where he whispered, "Pounding will commence now."

She giggled until he grabbed her ankles and sat back on his haunches. He put her feet on his shoulders, moved one of his feet to the floor, and entered her—swift, sure, and strong.

"Tattoo!" she gasped.

One hand traced below her breast, drawing an imaginary line. She was lost following the movement, overwhelmed by the sensations. Drunk on Hudson. It sounded like the name of a bar near the river.

"I can't hold back," he urged, slipping his thumb to her clit. He didn't rub or massage. He just pressed and let the rocking motion of his body do the work.

The lights got brighter, the air crisper, and her body tighter as the orgasm barreled through her like the subway beneath them.

He cried out her name, and she knew then and there that no matter what happened, he'd tattooed her that day. It was permanent; she would never be the same. He was getting to her, making her think she could actually do the things she'd dreamed about—be someone bold and free. She'd had him between her legs now, what else could she do?

**Verity Michaels @VerityPics03**
Couch yoga FTW. #HanesProvocateur #Pounded

**Verity Michaels** @VerityPics03
Maybe it's the cock talking, but I think my common sense got knocked out of place.

**Verity Michaels** @VerityPics03
Or maybe into place?
#PoundSense #NewWomanNewPerspective

# Chapter 13

Dating for Dummies
Debra Anastasia

After a few more weeks of research, Verity was able to conclude that she liked sex with Hudson. Okay, she loved sex with Hudson. He knew so much about her vagina that she wondered if he planned to produce the definitive work. And outside the bedroom, they'd developed a pattern. He would wait for her after work on the days he delivered in her part of the city, and she would listen to his stories. He would tell her where he'd been and pass her songs he thought she'd love. Some nights he was busy, and he was vague as to why. But when he was all hers? He was all hers. Their weekends were adventures in Manhattan and the surrounding boroughs. Hudson seemed determined to make her a functioning city girl. They traveled by subway or walked on their own feet most of the time.

It seemed he knew people everywhere. He was affable and friendly, but those they encountered seemed to give him his space after saying hello. Maybe it was Verity's presence. She had continued to wonder if she wasn't the only one in his life. His periodic nighttime scarceness was a constant topic for her and Angie, but Verity remained too worried about seeming untrusting to ask him about it.

However, the weekend of her birthday turned out to be one of those Hudson-scarce times. So she and Angie had met out on Saturday, after Angie ditched Joseph, for a girls' night.

"So, I mean, you've been with him for a few months now. I think it's time to claim that salami." Angie wrinkled her nose. "You could put a nametag through the piercing."

Verity shook her head. She had shared the details of Hudson's special decorations with Angie, but now that her friend brought it up all the time, Verity was kind of wishing she hadn't.

"I hate the idea of pushing him into making this more than he's ready for. I mean, we bag the noodle, if you know what I'm saying." Verity gave Angie an exaggerated wink.

"No one calls putting a condom on a penis that," Angie snorted.

"Okay, but, like, tonight's my birthday, right? We have a lot of fun together, but we keep it pretty light. He seems like he wants to get to know me, but he's so mysterious, I feel weird bringing up stuff about myself. Soooo, I didn't exactly tell him about today. I put his nuts in my mouth, which means I should've been able to do that, but I didn't. I'm not expecting a hot dog with a candle in it." Verity scanned the bar as she exhaled her disappointment.

"How did you celebrate birthdays in Florida? Oh, wait!" Angie gave Verity a low whistle. "Speak of the noodle now…"

Verity followed her gaze, and saw Hudson smiling his way

into the bar.

"Hey, Honeybee! I heard it's your birthday. I'm so sorry for not knowing this. You have to tell me!" Hudson pulled a crushed rose out of his hoodie pocket.

Verity took it and lifted her eyebrow. "This flower looks like it's been dead three weeks. And I'm very careful about sharing personal information. You know, identity theft is a real concern. Slap a wig on you, and you could be applying to rent a forklift in my name." Hudson looked mildly confused, but Verity barreled ahead. "Who told you?"

Angie fake coughed, and Verity gave her a look.

"What? I'm a great sneaky tweeter. He needed to know." Angie kept looking at Hudson's crotch.

"Can I join ladies' night? Is that okay?" Hudson pulled up an empty chair.

"Sure. As long as you can confirm you aren't porking anyone but my sweet friend here." Angie squealed as Verity slapped her in the arm.

Hudson laid on his usual sparkling charm and changed the topic. After a couple more rounds—of both drinks and attempted inquisition from Angie—he ordered an Uber car and insisted on paying for Angie's ride.

"I like to make sure all the ladies get home safe." Hudson held the car's door for Angie as she got in outside the bar.

After saying goodbye and silently promising to pinch Angie the next time she saw her, Verity was alone with Hudson.

"So, do *you* have any questions?" He wrapped his fingers around her hand and interlaced his colorful knuckles with her plain ones.

"A few. Maybe. But I'd prefer you tell me what you want to

at your own pace." Verity touched his knuckles and didn't meet his eyes.

"You know what? Can we go to my place? I think I can answer a lot of your questions there." Hudson gave the driver directions after she nodded.

On the way, Verity felt like her eyelids had a heartbeat, she was suddenly so anxious. Hudson's mystery had allowed her to invent excuses for him, instead of determining he was thoughtless. Or married. Maybe he was a spy? Their Uber car pulled up in front of a gold-plated building she knew was too expensive for a bike messenger, and yet it stopped. Dear God, did he live with his parents? Hadn't he said they lived elsewhere? After he paid the driver, Verity gave him a skeptical look.

"Are we breaking into somewhere else, Tattoo? I swear you're determined to give me a Felony Ever After." She hugged herself.

"What? Instead of a Happily Ever After? Why you got to do me like that, Country Girl?" He pulled her into his arms, sliding his hands under her jacket and into the waistband of her jeans. He lifted his chin as he embraced a fake thug persona that she kind of wished he would pull out in the bedroom.

"I like to think I do you pretty good," she countered. "Remember the last time when I hit your nuts with the vibrator as you came?"

He clamped his hand over her lips and gave her a two-dimple smile. "Yeah. I remember. That was a master-class move, baby. But maybe my doorman doesn't need to know that about me." He spoke in a whisper and gave a pointed look to the hip-looking guy who Verity would never have guessed was a doorman.

But he did indeed hold the door open for them, and he addressed Hudson as *Mr. Fenn.*

Hudson produced a card that allowed him access to the elevator, and they stepped inside. She looked at him like he was juggling dragons. "You really live here?"

"I do. I do." He hit a button and looked her up and down. "I love elevators." His tongue peeked out of his mouth, and he bit his bottom lip.

Verity narrowed her eyes. "Don't distract me with your sex face. Tell me how you live here? Do you squat with your parents? And was that your hipster doorman?"

The elevator pinged, and he held the door open for her. "It's a new model of building management geared to us young folk—the up and comers."

He dragged out the word *comer*, and Verity rolled her eyes. "So you can get a place in this building as a bike messenger?"

"You have a lot of questions." He unlocked the door.

"It's my birthday. I think answers can be my gift." Verity followed him into the dark space.

"I got you a flower." He slapped on the lights.

"It was dead." She was going to joke around more, but lost her train of thought when she saw the inside of the apartment. It was so outside the realm of what she was expecting, she knew her jaw was hanging open. "This is you? Right now? In this life you live here?"

Verity wanted to look around, but his arms and mouth had better ideas. He lifted her and carried her as she clung to him, kissing with naughty intentions. The next thing she knew, she was in his semi-dark bedroom, and he'd tossed her on the bed.

His scent, the very Hudson-ness of his clothes, was

embedded in the room. He looked bashful, and a bit frantic, as he surveyed the space. He took a minute to gather up the clothes strewn on the floor. It wasn't a crazy mess, just an indicator of a busy morning, maybe. Verity propped his pillows against his headboard and crossed her legs at the ankle.

She watched as his confident demeanor took a few minutes off. She liked sheepish Hudson.

"I'm sorry it's not neater. You were a surprise tonight. But I didn't want to miss your birthday after I got that news." He pulled his leather jacket off and tossed it on the chair in the corner.

He was wearing a white tank tucked into his jeans, a look she'd never seen him rock before. He noticed her taking inventory, and he pulled off the tank, revealing his abs underneath.

"I just grabbed my jacket. Didn't want to wait even a minute to get to you."

Verity patted the spot next to her on the bed. "Come here."

He gave her a glimpse of the dimples, and she enjoyed how his bare arms looked as he got in position next to her. The muscles rippled, and his collarbone flexed.

"How much did you drink?" He propped up next to her and held her hand again, lifting it to his lips for a kiss.

"Not enough. I'm not drunk; I just want more of you." Verity watched his full lips as he decided to grace each of her knuckles with its very own kiss.

"You can have all of me, baby." He switched his attention from her knuckles to her face, but she put up her index finger to halt the kiss he clearly intended.

"No. I want more of this." She placed her other hand on his

chest. "What's inside. What makes Hudson a tattooed, bike-riding parkour enthusiast who gives a country girl the time of day?"

"You're already in my place. Isn't that enough?" He tried to kiss her again.

"Nope. Tell me about you. The tattoos. Why cover yourself in them?" Verity had pulled away a little, but kept her hand in his and her other on his chest.

"You hatin' the tats?"

"You're defensive tonight. I love the tattoos. I could lick all of them all day and not get bored. The one on your stomach? That's breakfast, lunch, and dinner. Just tell me why. I mean, you've got ink on your knuckles, neck, and everything in between. That's a big commitment to make at a pretty young age. And I don't think you did it to be trendy. They seem like meaningful shit."

"Meaningful shit? That poetry should be published. How about I just show you what these pictures look like moving over your goddamn gorgeous body?" He came at her again, his hand finding her breast. "Sometimes at night I picture piercing this." He found her nipple easily through her thin shirt and lace bra. "And it makes me rock hard."

She pushed him away, panting. "Stop distracting me. Tell me about the tattoos."

Hudson swore under his breath. He sat next to her and adjusted himself. She almost felt bad for the amount of arousal he was trying to keep in his jeans.

"You're in my bed, and this is what you want?" Hudson put his hands behind his head.

Verity nodded, not trusting herself to use words. She was

pretty sure she would chant *dick* a few hundred times if she opened her mouth anyway.

"Okay. I got my first tattoo at seventeen. To honor my mom." Hudson hadn't talked much about his parents, so this was a first, and it sobered her penis-addled brain.

She left the silence between them as an invitation. He pulled out his phone and flipped through his pictures. He finally passed her the device.

The woman in the picture smiled beneath a blond beehive. She had the same dimples as Hudson. She was in a wheelchair; her head listed to the side.

Verity nodded at this image of his past, not sure what to say.

"She passed away two weeks after that picture was taken. She had ALS. She loved that crazy wig."

Verity looked at his face, but he was still looking at the picture.

"I'm so sorry." Verity looked at the picture again. And true enough, his mother had dark circles under her eyes, and her arms were too thin.

"She was my everything. And you'd never guess it—she always hid it—but her arms, her legs, her back? Covered in gorgeous tattoos. She stayed covered up, though. A sweater, long-sleeved tops in summer. She never went swimming. I thought she just didn't like it. I didn't know she had them until I helped her after she started experiencing symptoms. First was tripping, then dropping things. Do you know they can't diagnose ALS? They can only eliminate everything else."

Verity ran her fingertips down his forearms before shaking her head. "Lou Gehrig's disease, right? I've never known anyone else who had it."

He nodded slowly. "It's a bitch. A vicious bitch of a disease—degenerates nerve cells in the brain and spinal cord."

Verity felt her eyes fill up.

"Her muscles went slowly at first, but with a predictable decline, they failed her. And my father—the man who'd promised her until death did them part—wouldn't help her. He said it hurt him too much to see her losing herself. He didn't even care that it was still her inside—maybe even more amplified because it was like she was a concentrated version of herself. If he'd let himself, he would have seen the beauty in helping her. I could see it, and I was just a teenager. The fight in her. She fought to bike every day until she fell off for the fourth time. Then she got a stationary bike."

"That was heartless of him." Verity felt the words slip out. She couldn't even fathom what that kind of diagnoses would do to a family dynamic.

His jaw and neck tensed. "Well, good ol' dad? He runs a vitamin company. And not just any vitamin company. The one that promises to ward off cancer and other disease. So my mom getting ALS? She made him look bad. He's a charlatan who claims vitamins can make you live forever. So his wife wasn't allowed to be anything but perfect. Wholesome. No tattoos, no diseases, no weakness." He shook his head. "He didn't understand that she was the strongest person in the world. So much stronger than him."

Verity touched Hudson's neck, then his jaw. She had no words, but she could listen.

"He divorced my mom. So he could distance himself from what she was going through."

She felt her mouth drop at the audacity.

"Oh yeah. He's an asshole." Hudson picked up his phone with the image of his mom on the screen.

"So I had to wheel her into divorce court and translate for her because they couldn't understand her speech anymore—you had to be around her every day to understand her, you had to be used to her. The day after that she had me call her tattoo artist. Spring Felt was her name. She tattooed a bike on my mom. She had a bike squeezed in between all these beautiful tattoos, and she told me to keep on getting on any bike I fell off of. That's what she wanted to leave me with."

Verity saw the outline of a bike on Hudson's arm, and she traced it.

"I got this at seventeen, the day after my mother's funeral. My father thought that after I was done caring for his wife—doing the things a husband should have done to help her survive, to help her stay as comfortable as possible—he thought then I would want to go to college and take over his vitamin empire. I was required by the courts to live with him until I was eighteen, and I got as many tattoos as Spring would give me. I made him look at them. He wanted a wholesome heir. I was determined to give him a thug."

"And that's what I assumed you were when I met you. I'm so sorry."

"It's okay. I forgive you. They're my favorite disguise. My protection."

He ran his hands through his hair.

Verity shifted so she could straddle him. She held out her arms.

He leaned forward and accepted her hug. She kissed the top of his head.

"You're a beautiful son. I bet she's so proud of you."

Hudson wiped at his face and hugged her back. "Yeah. So that's why the tattoos. Lots. Everywhere. She hid them from my dad, so I made sure he had to look at them on me."

Verity hugged him hard again and then placed her hands on his jaw, lifting it so she could kiss him.

"Thank you."

"You need to know anything else?"

"Not tonight. Now I want to see all those tattoos in motion again."

Hudson was tender this time. Gentle. And when they came, they were looking into each other's eyes.

Verity dreamed of a warmth and comfort she could never quite capture, and in the morning, she woke up in a twisted knot of limbs. She could tell from Hudson's dead weight and even breathing that he was still asleep. She stroked his hair gently. He'd been through so much, and it must have taken a lot for him to finally open up a little last night. He was his mother's only child, though he had a good relationship with the younger half-sisters his father had gone on to create with two other much younger women. She felt honored that he'd shared this with her, but Hudson's heart-wrenching story didn't explain where he went from time to time. And she felt like an intruder asking that now. He seemed to need some mystery, and maybe that was okay.

When her phone started pinging, she remembered she'd scheduled a highly coveted hot yoga class with Angie this morning. There was no missing it.

Verity got dressed with "help" from Hudson, who tried to slow her down with kisses and gropes. She didn't even have time to tour the apartment, though she could tell it was spacious and likely full of interesting things. On her way out, she was looking for her shoes and tried what she thought was a closet. Hudson caught her hand before she could open the door.

"What?" Verity thought he was trying to distract her again.

"Your shoes are over there." He pointed at the couch, but kept his hand on the knob.

"What's in there?" She put her hand flat on the door.

"I thought you were late?" Hudson put his distracting body between her and the room she was curious about now.

"And I thought you were trying to get me to stay?" Verity narrowed her eyes.

"I am. In there." He nodded toward the bedroom. "Not in here." He tapped the door in question with the back of his head.

Verity's phone pinged again. She had to go. She was going to be even later than she was.

"I'll have the doorman call you a car." Hudson tapped his lips with his finger.

She hesitated a moment, but then remembered the vulnerable man who'd fallen asleep in her arms last night and gave him a pass. For now.

She gave him a lingering kiss and hurried to her shoes.

He held the front door open for her, and she made sure to swing her hips a little extra for his benefit.

**Verity Michaels @VerityPics03**
And then he changes everything with his beautiful heart.

#HuggingHim

**Hudson Fenn** @tatwhiteknight
You bring out the best in this crazy old organ. #YoureBeautiful

# Chapter 14

### Splinters
### Katherine Stevens

After a fabulously sweaty session of hot yoga and an even hotter shower at the gym, Verity parted ways with Angie and took herself on a special birthday shopping trip on the way home. She'd calculated carefully, and she deserved it.

Back at her apartment, she surveyed her haul for a moment and then knew exactly what to do.

Hudson answered on the first ring. "What's up, Honeybee?"

The flip-floppy thing her stomach did at the sound of his voice hadn't changed since this morning. "Actually, I have a favor to ask you."

"Does it involve grand theft auto?"

Verity sighed. "No."

"Do you want me to steal something smaller, like a bike?"

"No."

"A unicycle?"

"Also no. I bought myself a birthday present, and I want you to help me use it. Meet me in Washington Square Park in thirty minutes?"

"Please tell me your present is a unicycle. I'll see you soon."

Verity packed up her purchases and was sitting on the edge of the fountain exactly twenty-nine minutes later. A moment later she saw Hudson walking toward her, ink flowing from beneath every part of his short-sleeved shirt. Knowing why he'd chosen to get those tattoos made them even more beautiful.

When he reached her, Hudson pulled her to standing and kissed her firmly, finishing with a dip. "Now what's this about a favor?" He pointed to the case slung over her shoulder. "That doesn't look big enough for a unicycle."

"Let the unicycle go." Verity rolled her eyes as she unzipped the case, but couldn't stop smiling as she pulled out the camera. It felt so good in her hands. "I bought my camera back," she said, turning to face Hudson. "I've worked the receptionist job long enough to afford this, and I've realized I really missed it, even without the business. I'd like you to help me break it in."

Hudson kissed her again. "I like seeing you with a camera in your hands. You look happy. And you have some impressive miserly ways too. I'm so glad you're taking back this part of who you are." He looked around eagerly. "Am I your assistant? Do you want to take pictures of the park?"

Verity suddenly felt nervous. "Ummm... not exactly. I was hoping I could take pictures of your tattoos...in the park."

Hudson was silent for a moment—amazingly. "You want to take pictures of...me?"

Verity smiled. "I do. The light is perfect right now too. And when I'm done, you'll be able to add modeling to your résumé."

Hudson rubbed his chin, feigning deep thought. "The

Messaging Model? That's got a nice ring. I like it. Snap away!"

She led him to a group of trees and found him a comfy spot in the grass. Then she created image after image of the designs and pictures on his arms. She wanted to ask him about every single one, but the park seemed too open and exposed for such a conversation. She did, however, coax him out of his shirt for a little while.

As she photographed, following her instincts and letting the details catch her eye, Verity felt a number of conflicting emotions she couldn't quite explain. She'd forgotten what it felt like to capture beauty with the proper equipment, to transform a moment in time into something permanent. And Hudson was so beautiful. She could see that now—so alive and fierce and vibrant. How had she ever dismissed him as a criminal? He turned to stick his tongue out at her. She swallowed the lump that formed in her throat.

At the end of their session, she laced their fingers together and photographed their hands, just as she'd imagined doing.

"I think I've got enough for now," she told him after that, setting the camera back in its case. "Do you want to come back to my place for a drink? I can hook this up to my laptop and show you what I did."

Hudson stood, pulling his shirt back over his head. "I'm all yours. Lead the way."

They held hands on the short walk back to her apartment, but they didn't talk much. Perhaps Hudson was saving his energy because the second they walked through her door, he spun her around and pulled off her shirt.

"Your turn to be topless!" he announced, and Verity needed little convincing. They jettisoned their remaining clothes faster than a plane trying to break the sound barrier.

They were soon a pile of sweaty limbs on the hardwood floor of her living room. She knew they'd be sore the next day, but neither seemed interested in breaking their connection long enough to move to the bedroom.

A little while later, after nearly being drilled into Mrs. Beatman's apartment one story below, Verity really wanted to be that girl who could say something sexy. But she wasn't that girl.

"There's a twenty on the dresser for you." *Not even close to being that girl.*

Hudson shifted to look her in the face. "Excuse me?"

Verity giggled. At least she'd been able to throw him off balance. That was a nice change of pace. He laid on top of her while they caught their breath.

"I'm kidding," she said. "But I do need to get up."

She helped him to his feet as well. "Can I get you something to drink like I originally promised? I'm not a very good hostess."

"I'm not complaining," Hudson said. "This beats the reception I get at most places."

Verity looked down at the spot on the floor where they'd just had sex. It was buffed and shinier than the rest. Perhaps they could make the rest of the floor match it over time. Her apartment wasn't very big, so it wouldn't even take that long.

She went to the kitchen, rubbing her sore backside as she went. It was a good hurt though. Or actually, no. *No, this is a bad hurt. Ow.*

Verity jogged to her bedroom to look in the mirror. Oh, boy. And it had been such a magical day…

"Everything all right?" Hudson called from the couch.

She was woefully unprepared for this situation. Requiring help with an intimate area in broad daylight seemed like it should involve a co-pay. Would Hudson be up for this? Would she survive the mortification? She looked in the mirror at different angles, as if the problem might have been caused by a fun house mirror or a trick of the light. No such luck.

She looked back and forth between the mirror and the couch where her unsuspecting visitor sat. They were close now, right? Closer. She knew about his mom. It was time for her to share this side of herself. The backside. Her backside.

Her tattooed lover craned his head around the door frame. "Honeybee, is everything okay?"

She was out of options now. Smiling her bravest smile, she asked, "How are you with splinter removal?"

The expression on Hudson's face went from confused to whatever emotion comes after really confused. "Come again?"

"I don't think I can." Verity looked at the rug under her feet. If only she had rugs in the living room.

"You've really lost me now."

She exhaled the last of her dignity. "Splinters. I've got splinters in my behind from when I was being hashtag pounded by Hudson!" She took another breath. "I can't get them out myself. Will you help me?"

It seemed to take him a few tries to put together a thought. "You very willingly put my penis in your mouth—not to mention bossing me around as your photo subject all over the park—yet you're having trouble asking for my help? When did you get so shy?"

"When I got splinters in my ass. Are you going to help or not?" The dread of what was to come made her hostile.

A mischievous grin spread across Hudson's face. "What's it worth to you?"

"Oh, you've got to be kidding me!" Verity sat down on her bed with a dramatic huff and immediately bounced back up with a yelp. "Okay, fine! What do you want?"

"Another date," he said with a hint of a question.

"Another date?" she repeated with far more than a hint of a question.

"Yes. Another date with my *girlfriend*." He tried to look serious, but burst into a smile.

Despite the pain in her nether regions, Verity couldn't help but smile too. She resisted the urge to make a joke about his niece. "Are you really bargaining with me to be your girlfriend?"

"I don't think you're in any position to bargain, Honeybee. I say we just go with it." When she nodded, feeling a blush warm her cheeks, he rubbed his hands together. "Now, how about we take a closer look at that spectacular ass of yours?"

Verity held up a finger and trudged to the bathroom to retrieve her tweezers. When she returned, Hudson was sitting on her bed, looking like the cat who ate the canary. The pain in her butt felt slightly anesthetized by his use of the word *girlfriend*. It gave her a very middle-school thrill.

He put out his hand. "Tweezers."

She placed them in his open palm.

"Scalpel."

"This isn't really that funny, you know."

Hudson tried to cover his laughter with a cough. "Can I make one joke about you being full of wood? Please?"

Verity giggled in spite of herself. "No! Just get these freaking splinters out of me!"

"Your wish is my command." He patted his legs. "Lay across my lap."

She laid face-down, hoping to suffocate in her embarrassment.

"This is kind of like playing that Operation game," he said after a moment. "I was always pretty good at that. Can you make a buzzing sound from time to time?"

"That's not helping..." Verity tried for her best warning tone.

Hudson snorted. "I disagree. They say laughter is the best medicine, and I'm feeling great!" He ruffled her hair. "All right, I think I'm all done with that side. Flip around so I can take care of the other cheek."

Verity repositioned, and Hudson kissed the center of her back. "You're beautiful, Verity. This is my favorite new game. We are never sanding that floor."

Her teeth remained clenched, but she soon found that to be more trouble than it was worth. While not exactly enjoyable, this was certainly not the worst experience she'd had with a man. She prepared herself for pain that never came. What was he doing back there? She twisted her head to look at her tattooed Florence Nightingale, only to find him staring quizzically at her wounded rump.

"What's this?" he asked.

"What's what?"

"You have a mole on your left cheek. I've never noticed it before."

"Oh, that. Yeah, I got it for my birthday when I was born." Verity had no idea why anyone would be so fixated on this. It was a tiny mole, not a third arm growing out of her ass.

"It's heart-shaped."

"That it is." She felt another blush creeping over her with all the scrutiny, but before she could encourage him to get back to work, she found herself unceremoniously dumped onto her bedroom floor. *What the—?*

Hudson stood above her, unbuttoning his jeans. He was suddenly in the mood for another round right now? Her mole had magic powers...

"Look!" Hudson mooned her like a fraternity pledge during Rush Week. And there it was: a little heart-shaped mole on his right buttock. It was so small compared to the veritable bonanza of tattoos across his magnificent body, she had completely overlooked it.

They were tooshie twins. Caboose compadres. Butt buddies, if you will. This was a tiny piece of him, matched perfectly to a tiny piece of her. He'd had this mark his whole life, just waiting to find its counterpart. It was all too much to process, so Verity said the only thing you can say after realizing you might have met your soulmate.

"Do you want to go grab some breakfast for dinner after you finish pulling the splinters out of my behind?"

**Verity Michaels** @VerityPics03
Mole butties with my boyfriend. #NotAwkward

**Verity Michaels** @VerityPics03
I have a boyfriend. #ThatsAnUpdate

**Verity Michaels** @VerityPics03
Is he too old to buy a varsity jacket with his name on it so I can steal it? #HighSchoolGoals

# Chapter 15

### The Box
### Katherine Stevens

Verity rushed into work on the late side the next morning, but for the first time since she'd moved to the city, she had a real life outside her work—she was someone's girlfriend *and* an official photographer again—so that helped her calm her frazzled nerves. She'd no doubt have to deal with some grief from Mr. Lay, but she'd had a great morning, even though she was wearing her last clean and least favorite pair of remotely presentable panties.

She only did laundry when the basket was overflowing, and not a second sooner. The laundry facilities in her building left a lot to be desired. Like a miracle from a very strange bible, her laundry level had remained just below the basket's rim for some time now. However, her lingerie drawer had sneakily dropped to nearly empty.

As if she'd sensed Verity's arrival, Angie stepped out of the elevator, coffee in hand. "Look what the cat dragged in! Did hot yoga take everything you had, or was it an eventful evening?" Smiling, Verity patted her bum in response. "Oh, very eventful. Happy birthday weekend to me."

"Do tell," Angie breathed.

Before Verity could speak, Lay barreled into the lobby. He stopped abruptly and stood watching her, seeming almost transfixed. Finally he seemed to remember himself and tried to look nonchalant. "Verity, there's work to be done. I need you in my office immediately." He inclined his head toward her confidante. "Good morning, Angie."

Angie arched an eyebrow at him, combing her hair away from her face with her middle finger.

While Verity would have much rather stayed to chat with Angie, she also wanted to get Lay's agenda out of the way as soon as possible. She could take her lumps. As long as they weren't delivered to her backside.

The three endured an awkward elevator ride upstairs together—had the car somehow gotten smaller over the weekend? Larold's cologne was devastating—and Angie beelined for her office as soon as the doors opened.

Verity continued down the hallway with her boss, and when they reached his office—no Marge in sight—he closed the door behind her and directed her to a chair. This was going nowhere good. Larold Lay had a lot of cards in his playbook: He could talk her ear off until she lost the will to live. He could guilt her into staying at the office all night to do Marge's work. He could peek at her like a pervert for hours on end. Or, he could choose a combination move.

*Bring it*, Verity thought. *I'm a new woman today. My existence is more than this job. Also, I have a boyfriend. With a penis.*

Mr. Lay had turned his back to her, undoubtedly preparing his nefarious scheme, and he now spun to face her with a determined look in his eyes. He sat in the chair opposite hers and handed her an oval bowl filled with what appeared to be clay.

"Hold this."

*Well, this is new.* "What is that?" Verity felt a chill run through her. This was surely a trap. Maybe he was making a bomb and wanted her fingerprints on it. *Is that what's been in the boxes?*

"Did I ask you to question me?" Lay seemed more agitated than usual.

The prudent thing would be not to aggravate him further. But... "Why would you *ever* ask me to question you? That doesn't make much sense." Verity felt like being with Hudson had instilled a firmer backbone in her—along with his impressive other bone.

"Can you please just press your face in the clay?" Lay looked to be near tears.

"Do what? Are you crazy?" Verity's internal alarms went straight to panic. She batted the bowl out of his hand like a cat on meth.

Lay caught it as it soared through the air. "Don't get your brown panties in a wad! It's a face mask we're sampling for a client. Now put your face in the bowl!"

Verity shifted in a futile effort to find a more comfortable position for her butt. The fake leather seat rubbing against her pleather skirt sounded like two sea lions with bronchitis mating on a beachhead. "You have lost whatever was left of your mind if you think I'm going to—wait, how do you know my panties are brown?" She hopped off her chair abruptly, putting an end to the semi-aquatic mating song.

Lay shifted the bowl back and forth between his hands. "I—uh—I don't. It was a lucky guess."

"Bullcrap. How dare you look up my skirt?"

She thought he mumbled, "Research is research." But she wasn't completely sure.

Verity was still formulating a plan that involved shoving that bowl into one of Lay's orifices when the door to his office opened. There stood a bike messenger—and not her favorite one either. More like a cheap knock-off copy.

"There was no one up front, so I let myself in." The guy still had his earbuds in, so he spoke at least four times louder than necessary. The music pumping from him could be heard across the room. Under his right arm was another box.

Lay grabbed it from the messenger before Verity could get her fingers around it. He walked past her, whispering creepily. "Curiosity killed the cat, Verity."

For a moment she imagined punching Lay right in *his* package. He would drop the box in her lap as he crumpled to the floor. Then she'd say something clever like, *There's a twenty on the dresser for you.* But she didn't. She wanted to be a girl unafraid of consequences who went around punching jerks in their meat and potatoes, but she wasn't totally there. Yet.

Still, she at least used the messenger's exit as an opportunity to escape. But she paused when he got on the elevator. He looked at her, holding the door open, while she contemplated her life. She had her camera back, and she'd landed a really great guy, but neither of those things would pay her rent next month. Verity waved the messenger on, and as the elevator door closed, she decided to take the high road and at least leave things on a professional note with Lay. The bowl of face mask thing was weird, but he was such an odd duck, maybe it made sense to him. She could just politely decline.

When she reached his office again, she knocked as she pushed open his door, which was slightly ajar, and caught the tail end of him opening his precious package.

Verity wasn't sure when she started screaming, or if she would ever stop. As Lay removed the last of the packaging, out popped a human arm that had been unnaturally contorted inside.

Lay jumped to his feet, waving his arms. "Will you be quiet? It's rubber; it's not real!"

This confused Verity enough to silence her. She stepped over to the appendage in question. It was indeed rubber, which almost made it creepier. She had a good mind to start screaming again. "What in the heck are you doing with a rubber arm, Lay?"

He glanced nervously at the door to his private bathroom, then back at Verity, and then back to the door. "Nothing."

Verity figured she might as well go for broke at this point, since her version of being professional didn't even remotely seem to fit in this fun house. She charged the bathroom before Lay could stop her. As soon as she opened the door, someone started screaming again, and Verity was pretty certain it was her.

In front of her stood a faceless, one-armed, one-legged life-size rubber doll—held together by Velcro, obviously having been constructed in pieces. Verity couldn't decide on the most horrifying facet until her eyes found the doll's adhesive name tag: *Hello, my name is Verity*. That's when the screaming stopped.

Verity swung around to look at the discarded bowl of clay on the floor, then back at her faceless doppelganger. "Sweet mother of frankincense, you were trying to make a mask." And thus started another round of screaming.

She did have enough of her wits about her to appreciate that the doll was wearing a beautiful set of glittered angel wings on its back—like a Victoria's Secret model created by Tim Burton.

"I'm going to need to know what the hell this is." Verity faced her boss.

**Verity Michaels** @VerityPics03
I need hazard pay for this job. #IDidntSignUpForThis

**Verity Michaels** @VerityPics03
Yesterday > Today. #TheDollHasMyName #GetYourOwnNameBitch

**Verity Michaels** @VerityPics03
Need a more reasonable way to make money. Like drug dealing or prostitution.
#ALittleRestForTheWicked

## Chapter 16

A Way Out
Bella Aurora

Discovering that your boss has made his very own version of you is not going to go well under any circumstances. Finding a rubbery Frankenstein-esque monster-lady in your boss's private bathroom—likely to be used for slap-and-tickle purposes—would have freaked anyone out. All things considered, Verity thought she'd handled it well.

However, the mask-making sent her over the edge.

*He wanted her face.*

And he still wasn't answering her questions. He looked a bit like he'd forgotten how to speak. Verity needed to jog his memory *stat*.

Before she quite knew what she was doing, she'd delivered a swift kick in the nuts to one Mr. Larold Lay. He landed on the carpeted floor with an *oomph*. It felt good. Well, to her at least.

"*Christ*, my dick," he whimpered, cupping what was left of him. "My beautiful dick."

Verity glanced back at her lifeless double and shuddered. But along with revulsion, she felt a calm clarity. Strange as they were, things made sense now. *Of course* her boss had been receiving boxes with latex body parts in them. And *of course* he was assembling them into a replica of her. He was just weird enough to have that fall neatly into place. However, Verity was also keen enough to know this was a game changer.

The tongue she'd almost always bitten as Lay's employee now felt quite loose. She dragged a chair over to him, still curled like a shrimp on the floor of his office. She sat primly as she could, wanting to maintain an air of class as she spoke.

"From the time I started working here, Larold—I can call you Larold, can't I?—you have made my life super weird. And I guess part of me always knew you were a little strange." She smiled. "But that—" She pointed behind them to the Madame Tussauds wannabe mannequin. "That is something else entirely. That isn't filed under quirky. That's filed under *seriously jacked up.*"

Verity sat taller, liking the position she suddenly found herself in, the power that buzzed through her like electricity. "I think I need a new job," she confessed to a quiet Larold Lay. "But I'm going to need this paycheck a little longer to make that work. Make sense, Larold?"

He was still for a long moment, but eventually nodded, his face rubbing on the carpet.

"In exchange for keeping quiet about the freakish sex doll you've been creating without my knowledge, I think I'll talk terms. Don't you agree?"

He nodded again, slowly, still curled up on the floor. Then he spoke quietly. "What do you want, Ms. Michaels?"

What did she want?
What did she *want*?
Holy hell in a handbasket. *That* was a loaded question.
What *didn't* she want? She thought of Hudson and felt brave, a laugh bubbling up.
"I want what vintage Dolly Parton wanted," she announced. At her boss's confused stare, she rolled her eyes. "Nine to five. Marge can do her own work from now on."
Lay nodded quickly, obviously happy with the terms. "Okay."
Verity chuckled. "Oh, no." She shook her head. "That's not quite all."
Shuffling around, Larold sat up on the floor, keeping his knees spread so as not to brush his bruised ding-a-ling. "Anything, Ms. Michaels," he said, offering his full attention.
"No more peeks at my chest," she began. "Or my freaking underwear. *Jesus*. If you drop another pen in front of me, I will find a place to put that pen, and I assure you, it won't be comfortable. Please treat me with the same respect you'd offer your mother. Additionally, if I come in a little late from time to time, or have a long lunch, cut me some slack like a decent human being. I get my work done. That's what matters."
He spoke through gritted teeth. "Is that all?"
Was that all?
Verity was stuck in a job she hated, working for a boss who creeped her out, all because the money was more than decent. She frowned. Was that all she was? Even her father would want more for her than that, wouldn't he? Or did she even care?
*Trapped, underappreciated receptionist* wasn't the person Verity thought she was, and it definitely wasn't who she wanted

to be. She wanted to be someone who worked to live, not lived to work. She wanted to be free to make her own decisions, use her brain, be creative. Have some fun! Yes, she had a New York apartment and a bit of money. It had enabled her to get her camera back. But for what purpose? Had she ever felt more alive than she did taking those pictures of Hudson?

Sadness washed over her. She rested her fingertips at her temples, massaging lightly. "What am I doing?" she muttered to herself.

Hudson's gorgeous face and tattooed neck came to mind, and Verity's heart smiled. *What would Hudson do?*

In that instant, her heart's smile took shape on her face. Standing, she looked down at her poor excuse for a boss and spoke sweetly. "I've changed my mind, Mr. Lay." She stood and turned away.

As her feet took her toward the door, she could feel Lay start to panic and struggle to stand. "Verity!" he called out. "Ms. Michaels!"

She paused at his office door, her hand already gripping the handle. She looked over her shoulder and beamed. "I quit," she told him. She felt a humongous load lift off of her shoulders, and she chuckled to herself when she heard Lay's stunned voice as the door closed behind her.

"You're not going to tell anyone about this," he said. Then after a pause, he added, "Are you?"

Without breaking stride, Verity sailed to the elevator and returned to her desk downstairs. It was funny how quickly she could pack her work life into a banker's box, and the items inside weren't even important.

Verity held her head high, her box under her arm, and smiled as she said goodbye to the co-workers who happened past her desk. Angie popped out of the elevator and looked down at the box under Verity's arm. Her eyes widened. "What happened?"

Verity smiled. "I quit."

Angie seemed confused, but she smiled. "I can't go for drinks at ten in the morning, but know that I will be in touch." She raised her hand for a high-five as Verity breezed past.

Verity smiled all the way out of the building and maintained that smile even as she maneuvered with her box down the subway stairs. She was able to step right onto her train and find a seat. She took this as verification from the universe that she'd made the right decision. She closed her eyes and laughed softly.

She was free.

Verity texted Hudson:

> You'll never guess what I just did.

He responded:

> At your ridiculous office, the possibilities are endless.

Verity smiled.

> It's not my office anymore. I'll be officing from home now.

His reply was quick.

> No kidding? Let's celebrate! I'll add your new office to my delivery route today. See you as soon as I can.

Hudson followed his text with her picture of the honeybee he'd sent himself back when they were getting to know each other.

She wasn't home ten minutes before her office box was unpacked, implements scattered on her coffee table: A scented candle. A mini cactus. A half-eaten chocolate bar from the day before. A mug from Angie that read, "Don't go bacon my heart," with two squiggly pieces of bacon underneath it. And a stolen office stapler, because truly, she'd earned it.

The knock on her front door spread a welcome smile on her face like icing on a cake. She could *so* use a beautiful, toe-curling orgasm from Hudson right now. She was so taken with that idea that she flung open the door without first looking through the peep hole.

Larold Lay put his body in the doorway, making it impossible to slam in his face. Dammit! What had she been thinking? Hudson never used her front door...

"Get out!" Her hands started shaking as the impropriety of his presence forced her to fear for her life. Sure, Larold had always been a little socially awkward and creepy, but the Verity mannequin indicated he might actually lack any common sense. And now he'd followed her home. He wasn't a weirdo, he was a predator! Verity could feel herself hyperventilating.

"Can you hear me out for one minute?" he begged. "I'm in no condition to do anything except beg for your forgiveness." He waved a hand at his ginormous crotch.

"Good God! What the hell?" She backed away in revulsion, unwittingly allowing him to enter her apartment.

"It's an ice pack. For my man business. Listen, I understand you've quit. And I know what I was doing looked crazy." His eyes darted to hers for a moment, and he put one palm on his chest—perhaps to indicate how heartfelt his words were? His other hand settled across his genitals, maybe to express his continued fear of her.

"Crazy would look like a winning lotto ticket compared to the shit show I experienced in your office." Verity crossed her arms over her chest and tried to use her peripheral vision to scope out any nearby home decorations that could be used as weapons.

Lay stepped closer.

"Do not close that door or so help me God I will scream so goddamn loud you'll wish you were dead." She pointed to his hand at the edge of her front door. "And then I will make it so."

He sighed. "Okay, there's no great way to explain this to you without sounding like a creeper. But I'm not. I just love latex. The dolls are a way of life for me." Lay shifted from one foot to another. "They're a safe way to experiment in—"

She interrupted his speech, stomping her foot. "Knock it off! Stop. Good fucks out loud, you do not know how to take a hint. Hopefully the restraining order I filed on the way home will teach you to shut your noise-making face hole."

It was a lie, but damn, she *would* file one—if she lived through this encounter. So she hoped it was more of a prediction than a lie.

"You didn't stop; I followed you," he countered. "I know. I know that makes it sound worse. But for right now, for your own safety, I'm going to confide in you so you know the truth. And you can yell, throw things, whatever, but my conscience is clear when I leave here today. I'll have told you everything I know." Lay gave her a very determined look. "That bike messenger you like so much is a problem. Has a problem. Is a problem."

Verity rolled her eyes.

"No, wait. Seriously. Okay, so I like the company of latex companions, and yes, the one you saw today was supposed to be you. But—"

Verity flailed her arms, and he began speaking as fast as an auctioneer.

"I like women at work, and I like latex, so I found a company online that custom makes the dolls. First you build the body according to precise measurements, then you send them a cast of the face, and five months later you get a gorgeous, hand-painted sex doll that you get to keep and dress however you'd like, and they just love you forever."

Verity felt a little nauseated. "You have more than one of these?"

He nodded eagerly, seeming oblivious to her horror. "These dolls are supposed to be one of a kind, but when I went to a doll-lovers convention in Las Vegas with some of my buddies—we call ourselves Humpers of Pumpers—I found out there'd been at least three more Paulines made. She's *my* beauty. I created her with my own hard work. The company's one-of-a-kind promise was a total lie." He was agitated, like a petulant child.

"Pauline from accounts receivable?" Verity had once heard that Lay had dated Pauline.

He nodded, and had the decency to look sheepish about it.

"So the creepy sex-doll makers made extra Paulines. Did she know you made the first one?"

"Yes. Absolutely. You're the only doll I've ever tried to make without my lover being in on it. Many women find it very flattering—and a threesome with themselves? Well, that just adds to the appeal." He winked at her, then seemed to think better of it and pretended to wipe at his lashes as if something was in his eye.

"How many dolls have you had this company make?" *Why am I asking these questions?*

"Well, you would have been the fifth."

"And the first non-consenting employee to model for your latex pleasure?" Verity had no idea why Lay seemed intent on telling her all of this horrible, nightmare-inducing information. "I could sue the living shit out of you."

"Please, no. Look, I realize now it was a mistake not to have your permission. I just have to tell you this. Then you'll understand. Here's the thing: that bike messenger. I think he's the reason the company is making the girls into mass-produced products. I have a bad feeling about him. He knows how particular I am. I have a very good eye for aesthetics—hence all the pens you picked up. I was researching the curve of your calf. The gentle slope of your bum—"

"You need to knock that off right now."

"I'm sensing that." Lay put up his hands and took a small step backward.

"Your conspiracy theory does not make any sense, nor does it defend anything you've done. You're trying to blame my boyfriend because he delivered a few of your crazy boxes? You're out of your goddamn mind." Verity ran for the couch and grabbed her phone only to watch it flicker once before the battery died. She heard Lay close the front door behind him.

"Listen, I'm not done," he said. The floor creaked as he made his way closer.

"You are so, so done, Larold. Like, history." She pretended to dial on her blank phone while she begged her racing heart not to explode.

"Okay, is your boyfriend... secretive? Is his family rich? Like, not my kind of rich, but richer?"

"Richie Rich?"

"Yes. Because I think his uncle owns the company that makes the dolls. All of us latex lovers are a very tight-knit group. Super tight. Like a fist—a fist with a little moisture."

Verity stepped up and slapped him across his stupid face. He nodded.

"I deserve that; I get carried away. I just love the dolls." Lay stepped backward, hands in the air.

"I'm getting a sense of that." She pretended to speak to a 911 operator. "Yes, hold please. Either this intruder will get to his point or I'll have you send the SWAT team over to staple his balls to his shoulders.

"Hudson Fenn is the nephew of Bill Janpo, owner of HoneyBee Enterprises. The dolls are called HoneyBees. Because they're so sweet. And you stick your prick in them."

She sat down hard on the couch. "That doesn't even make sense. Bees prick *you*. And how do you know anything about Hudson? All he did was deliver a few lousy packages."

"Like I said, we're a close-knit community. Or we were. I've been betrayed, and I can't rest until I stop whoever's making these extra dolls." He pouted, sitting next to her on the couch. "But we have to proceed carefully. I don't want to spook them and ruin my chance. We need to protect the one-of-a-kind dolls," he added, reaching out to clutch her arm. "They're my designs. For me. And only me."

"What do you mean *we*?" Verity whispered, removing his hand from her arm with a shudder. "You're still making no sense, and also, I quit, remember?"

"Well, fine. But has Fenn been paying really close attention to your vagina?" Lay asked, taking the conversation officially to the funny farm. "Almost like he was inspecting it?"

Verity slapped him again and pointed to the door. "Seriously. Out!" she commanded, moving to a safer spot across the room.

Lay stood, but kept talking. "That's the next thing HoneyBee is rumored to be working on. Vagina replicas." He nodded as if this were the most normal thing in the world. "I've heard they hired an MIT grad to perfect their design process."

*MIT? Where Hudson supposedly went?* Verity wasn't a fainter, but now Lay's words circled around in her head against a backdrop of her most private moments with Hudson. Could any part of this craziness be true? Before today, a latex copy of herself had seemed beyond the realm of possibility, but looky what Larold had in his office bathroom...

"Scientifically superior genitalia—I won't lie, that does appeal to me." Lay was still talking as if this were a subject she wanted to discuss. And he was still in her apartment. "Does Hudson have a space he keeps secret? Somewhere you're not allowed?"

When everything in her apartment started to blur, Verity knew she wasn't going to get Larold out before she checked out. She was going down. The last thing she saw was Lay looking at her oddly. Then black.

**Verity Michaels** @VerityPics03
Vagina Inspections will be in room three. Vodka chasers. #NightmareFuel

**Verity Michaels** @VerityPics03
Ever have one of those days where sex dolls make perfect sense? #NoMeNeither

# Chapter 17

Come Again
Debra Anastasia

Waking up in Larold Lay's arms was even more horrible than she could have imagined. Handsome as he was, his breath smelled like glue. His neck was sweaty, and beads of moisture had all lined up on the starched collar of his shirt like they wanted to jump ship.

He was massaging her back. Verity became a slapping machine the instant her consciousness fully returned. "You Barbie doll-screwing fuck knob! Back up off me!"

He let her go, and she tumbled to the floor, her butt recognizing its old pal hardwood once again. She bounced up and swayed a bit. Fainting was weird shit.

Then Hudson climbed in her window. Like he always did.

"What the hell?" He looked wildly around the room, seeming completely unable to make sense of what he saw. Verity knew the feeling. He was so hot, and he looked so concerned. He couldn't be a dirty liar, could he?

Verity tried desperately to decide who to tell what. Her heart wanted to point at Lay and have Hudson beat him up, Power Puff Girl style, after she'd popped popcorn for the show. But her head knew she should find out if Lay's claims had any truth.

Her dilemma was solved when Lay stood, his huge groin looking even larger as he finally waddled toward the front door. "I'm leaving," he announced. "She fainted, so watch out for her." Lay waved his arms behind him, hitting parts of the wall and door before his hand found the doorknob. He twisted it frantically, never taking his eyes off Hudson.

Hudson advanced, and Lay scrambled to get out, shouting, "Don't forget what I said!"

Hudson turned back toward her when he reached the closed door. "Did he take your quitting really hard? Do I need to go kick his ass?"

Verity tilted her head and tried to memorize him. The testosterone, the offer to be her protector, the way his tattoo crept up his neck. She sat down on the couch after she felt the mental picture snap its shutter. "Thanks, but I think it's okay. I'll take a rain check, though."

Hudson sat next to her and pulled her close. He smelled magnificent. His weight on top of her might be the only thing that made sense at this moment.

"Honeybee." He massaged the back of her neck, but this time his nickname for her sent a chill through her body.

She shook him off and scooted away. He was a lot to take in her personal orbit. Everything seemed a bit much at the moment.

"What's wrong?"

"It's just, Lay said some things that upset me." She bit her index finger. *Is Hudson a liar?* She felt her heart drop to her stomach. *Is our whole relationship a lie?*

"That's it—he's going to learn what it's like to get pounded by Hudson too." He punched his fist as he stood, then seemed to realize his threat wasn't exactly as intimidating as he'd intended.

"Not sexually."

"I assumed," she assured him. "Anyway, what he had to say was about you."

"Come again?" His eyebrows knitted together.

"I wish it were that simple," she said, more to herself than him. "He said some crazy stuff. And I'm sure it's all lies, but I think I should ask you—"

"Okay, sure. I can't imagine what that guy could have to say about me that would affect you this way. I'm dying to hear it." He crossed his arms in front of his chest.

He didn't actually look that excited to hear it. Verity already knew sharing personal information was not Hudson's favorite thing. But she owed it to herself to be thorough, didn't she? They had to trust each other.

"Can you just answer one question? And I know it's off the wall, but…" She looked at her feet before regarding him again. "Does your uncle own a sex doll company?" She covered her mouth after she asked, almost literally closing the gate after the horses had escaped.

Hudson's face cycled through several emotions at once. Disbelief. "Really?" Indignation. "Really?" Disappointment. "Really. He does. That's what this is about? That's some sort of huge problem for you? I don't see how that affects us one bit. Your ridiculous boss came all this way to tell you that?"

He stood and headed toward the window.

"No! I mean, I was surprised, but that's not what I'm

worried—there's more to what he told me..." She stood quickly as the possibility the rest might be true as well loomed large. She swooned a little. This fainting was a real problem.

In an instant, Hudson's arms were around her. "Shit. Do you need to go to the ER?"

She touched her forehead with her fingertips. "I don't think I ate? Today has been such a whirlwind, and I had all that adrenaline from my triumphant exit. And then Lay was here... I bet it's just low blood sugar. You can go. We'll talk later. I'm sure this is nothing." She shook her head as he unwrapped his arms from her shoulders. She thought he was leaving, but instead he went to the kitchen to get her some orange juice.

She drank the whole cup.

"If that doesn't make you feel better, we're going to the ER." He sat in her armchair. "And I'm not going anywhere. When you're ready, tell me the rest."

Verity sat for a moment, then put the cup down when she felt stronger, wishing desperately to move past the weirdness.

"Are you okay?" He stood.

She nodded her head. "Better. I'll have a proper meal, and I bet I'll be fine. No worries." She stood and stayed sturdy on her feet to prove it to him.

"Good. Now tell me the rest."

Verity sighed, took a deep breath, and did her best to convey Larold's extra-sex-doll-copies conspiracy theory in a way that sounded as sane as possible.

It did not go well.

"I don't... I can't even... No way!" Hudson roared, his face a mask of controlled fury. "It's a reputable company—I mean, if you're into that sort of thing—not a pervert's free-for-all! And you think I would betray their clients' trust? I've got nothing to do with any of it except being related to the guy. You quit, and your crazy-ass boss—who had a *doll* made of you, yet another reason he needs an ass kicking—spews all this ridiculous crap on you, and you believe him? Over me? I thought we trusted each other."

Verity opened her mouth to speak, but had very little idea where to begin. She didn't want to be an idiot about things. She couldn't stand by and let someone lie to her. She'd seen how that turned out before. "I don't know what to tell you, Hudson. I'm just trying to understand all this."

"I'm going to give you some time to do that," he said.

He turned and slipped back out the window, and Verity watched instead of stopping him.

**Verity Michaels** @VerityPics03
Well, that was an unexpected turn. #Fainting #HoneyBee #Dolls

**Hudson Fenn** @tatwhiteknight
Trust before busts, I always say. #PlotTwist #PainHurts

# Chapter 18

Poor Decisions
Debra Anastasia

After she made herself some damn food, Verity spent the afternoon tweeting and attempting to sort through everything that had happened to her before noon that day. When Hudson failed to reappear in her window or respond to any of her tweets, she found her feelings on his part of the matter growing more and more disgruntled. He'd really been that pissy because she asked some questions? Clearly he'd never found a partially assembled latex version of himself in a boss's bathroom before. Probably another perk of being a bike messenger and renegade mysterious dude about town. And his relationship with his mother had obviously been very different than hers—starting with the fact that he had one.

Verity's flaky, lying mother was an artist. Well, that's what she claimed to be, but the splash canvases she specialized in didn't seem very emotionally deep. Maybe an explanation from the artist would make it all clearer, but Verity hadn't seen her since she was three. In her young mind she'd built her mother up to be a beautiful but busy princess.

Verity had held on to hope for her mother her whole childhood. She became a master at inventing excuses when she didn't show for visitation after promising the opposite. Verity would smile and let her father know it was okay while he seethed. The mumbling under his breath always continued for a few days after Verity had been disappointed.

Sometimes Verity wondered if she'd wished so hard for her mom to show up so her father would be happy. And as her childhood morphed into her teens, her heart had hardened toward her mom. She'd been even more angry when she realized her mother's irresponsibility and the pain it caused had ruined all types of art for her dad. Even after Verity showed him her business plan, he'd been extremely wary of her photography dreams. She'd wanted to prove to him that even though she liked to look at life through a lens, she could think like a business owner.

And then the business he'd helped her start, against his better judgment, had failed. She knew helping her find a job in New York City—the real business world—had made her dad feel relieved and confident in her future for maybe the first time since she'd finished college with a fine arts degree. Then she'd held on to that job for less than a year. Maybe she was as flaky as her mother had been.

She sighed. And as five o'clock rolled around, she decided she needed reinforcements.

She texted Angie:

> Please go to the liquor store and buy all the liquors right now.

Angie got her back almost instantly:

> On it. Legend. Big Ballo-Haver. Epic. #BossLevelBossShaming

Verity tried to clarify:

> Quitting is about one-tenth of what happened to me today. Vodkaaaaaaaa!

Angie sent her ten booze emoticons, followed by a series of question marks.

It was hard to find the right words, but Verity attempted it:

> Larold has a latex fetish and a doll that looks like me in his bathroom.

Then Verity added:

> Hudson is mad because I questioned him after Lay came to my house and said Hudson might be a rogue agent inside a sex doll company.

And then she added the cherry on the shit cake:

> A sex doll company owned by Hudson's uncle.

Angie didn't respond for a few minutes, and then the dots appeared that indicated she was typing.

> Are you having a stroke or something because that's the craziest series of texts ever.

Verity shook her head as she typed.

> I like that if I were having a medical emergency, we would text about it. I need you here with alcohol. Now.

Angie sent a picture of herself in the back seat of a car service.

Verity responded.

> Hooray! Please hurry. I'm getting started on the wine I use for cooking. Next up is rubbing alcohol.

The next picture was Angie holding up a stack of cash. Verity put her phone down, grabbed her biggest glass for wine, and upended the dregs of her cooking bottle.

Fifteen minutes later Angie unlocked the door with the extra key she had from watering the plants at Christmas. She was laden with bottles.

Fireball.

Tequila.

Wine.

Vodka.

"Those last two are from Joseph's cellar," Angie said proudly. "The good stuff. He never even lets me go in in there in case I wreck something." She lined the bottles up on Verity's coffee table.

That would cover all the hangover bases nicely. By the time they were done tonight, Verity would wake up wishing she wasn't human. She got out a nice glass for Angie to use as she wished.

Making sure her friend was seated, Verity then related her situation. They began her monologue with a couple of shots, and enjoyed a variety of drinks as the sordid tale unfolded: The sexy man stick of porn-gasms had called her his girlfriend less than twenty-four hours before her boss had confessed to being a weird sex maniac who was slightly obsessed with her, with a life-sized latex doll to prove it. Then she'd quit her job and her ex-boss had followed her home to accuse her newly statused boyfriend of sex doll industry misconduct. And then said boyfriend had been pissy *at her* about it.

When she'd finished, Angie sat back and seemed to struggle under the enormity of what had happened. "Okay, forget creep-ass Larold for the moment. You think sexy as sin Hudson is making knock-off sex dolls of women we work with, and also possibly a replica of your vagina?"

Verity pointed at her, choosing the Angie in the middle and noticing the room had begun to spin. "Yes. All of that." She made a wrap-it-up circle gesture with her fingers. "I think... Maybe... Or not, but I have to ask, right? He's so damn secretive, and I got a little freaked out. His uncle does own the company—HoneyBee. And Honeybee is Hudson's nickname for me to boot."

"That's overboard," Angie said. "Like, on the crazy train? That information dumped its load in my brain. I cannot comprehend that Hudson would be so devious. He seems so into you."

Verity poured another glass of wine. "I know. But he's all mysterious and shit. He's like Batman. We finally had a real talk about his family this weekend, but I still don't know where he goes when he disappears. I mean, it's okay to be private, but not to lead a double life."

Angie nodded. "I don't know, honey. I'm so sorry this happened. And on the Larold front, I can totally see why you quit, but I'll miss you so much at work."

"You're not quitting too?" Verity had hoped Angie might pack a box in solidarity, and perhaps to avoid becoming a sex doll in the future.

"I can't. I'm so sorry. I've put years into this company, and I have paid vacation coming up. I'll keep my mouth shut about what I know, but I'll have hawk eyes on Larold, and I promise to be a complete bitch to the girl that takes your place." Angie patted Verity on the arm.

"I'm unemployed. I'm unsure of my status with the hottest tattooed thief I've ever met, and there's a not-entirely-completed sex doll of myself in my ex-boss's bathroom." Verity sighed. "I gotta do something about this."

Angie touched her Fireball glass to Verity's wine glass. Verity sank down into her couch and pulled out her phone. No new messages from Hudson. No cute pictures. No calling her Honeybee, which she'd loved and now maybe hated.

She tapped on her Twitter app as Angie went into the kitchen to find food. Of course she stalked Hudson. She had no new mentions, but Hudson was tweeting his ass off.

**Hudson Fenn** @tatwhiteknight
You know when it's time to drink? Every time you click on her picture on your phone. #BottomsUp

**Hudson Fenn** @tatwhiteknight
I thought she trusted me. #AnotherOne

He was hurting. But really, he was a little fragile. Ugh, men. Damn him and his hot, tattooed, delicate-flower self.

Verity slammed back a Fireball shot and found the courage to tweet back. Angie reappeared with a plate of nachos and slid down next to her to assist.

**Verity Michaels** @VerityPics03
Honeybee my ass. #HudsonNeedsaPounding

    She didn't link it to him, but it gave her lady situation some happiness to see him tweet right at her. He was Twitter stalking her as well.

**Hudson Fenn** @tatwhiteknight
@VerityPics03 I would #Honeybee your ass allllll day. #HudsonWantsToPound

    "Oh, he didn't!" She looked at Angie with wide eyes.
    "You do ass stuff?" Angie replied with equally wide eyes.
    They giggled together before Verity responded, slurring a bit. "Not yet. But if we get through this, with enough lube and as drunk off my tits as I am now, I might consider it."
    Then Angie got all conversational, putting her hand over Verity's phone so she couldn't see the screen. "You know, I think if it was with someone I trusted, and I knew more about how to make that door more accessible? I might consider it too. I mean, Joseph is super interested in my thunderdome, but he hasn't wanted to get in there with his man hammer yet. If I put the no-no hole on the table, he might take the bait."
    Verity moved Angie's hand, ate a nacho, and refreshed the page. She probably needed to respond to what seemed to be

Angie telling her she and Joseph hadn't had sex yet, but the appropriate comment eluded her... if there even was one.

**Hudson Fenn** @tatwhiteknight
If I close my eyes right now I can see your ass in my head. #Splinters

She tried to find a comeback in her fuzzy head.

**Verity Michaels** @VerityPics03
If I close my eyes I see you tricking me into letting you into my life.

No hashtag, no joke. She'd accidently spoken her worst fear to him.

Angie bit her lip and hit refresh after reading Verity's response.

**Hudson Fenn** @tatwhiteknight
I've never tricked you. This isn't a game.

"Oh my God, are we having a fight on Twitter? This could not get any worse." Verity shook her head and tucked her phone in her bra. "What the hell were you just talking about?"

"Forget it. And forget him for a little while," Angie urged. "The only thing he needs to say is I'm sorry, and that's not going to happen on Twitter."

"Yes, screw this. If he wants to chat, let's do it in person." Verity stood and weaved a bit. Despite the nachos, there seemed to be plenty of free alcohol left in her system. Still, she was ready to roll.

She pulled her phone out of her bra and saw that Hudson's latest tweet was a picture of a beer on a table at the Library Bar. She flipped the phone to face Angie, who squinted and then nodded as a slow smile spread on her face.

"This is the best idea you've had all day. And you've had a ton of good ones. You are *so* the idea girl. Quitting your job? Great idea. Getting Lay to give you the latex replica of yourself? Stellar. Just gotta follow through. The excessive drinking? Also masterful. And now we're going to kick ass in person. I love it. Let's dress you up, though. We'll make Hudson's balls cry big, girly tears when he thinks of all the anal he could have had with you tonight."

"Did I tell you he has his tongue pierced? And his dick pierced?" Verity asked, holding Angie by her face. "Do you know what that means to a vagina? Are you aware of the commitment he's made to my vagina's happiness? He slapped his man meat out somewhere..." She waved a boozy hand at the city. "Thought about pleasure, and took a stab in his pee hole. Do you even understand that?"

"You did mention that already. And the tongue one is hard to miss." Angie nodded seriously. "Let's find the hottest thing you own and pour your boobs in it. Have I told you you have great tits? Your tits are the sweetest friends with my tits."

They proceeded to bump their boobs together.

"Okay, let's go." Angie dragged Verity to her closet.

**Verity Michaels** @VerityPics03
I've never thunk Fireball was a bad idea. #RageDrinking

**Verity Michaels** @VerityPics03
Angie made me sexlicious. #GreatTitBuddies

**Verity Michaels** @VerityPics03
Pierced dicks are fucktacular. #PoundTown

# Chapter 19

### Drunken Ninja Style
### Helena Hunting

Twenty-seven minutes and forty-two seconds later, Verity looked like getting laid was her main purpose in life. Angie had paired a hot pink micro-mini—which she'd worn last Halloween when she dressed up as the slutty pink Power Ranger—with a black lace thong.

On top, to compliment her skirt, was a silver sequined top with a deep scoop neckline. Verity looked like she was hiding two disco balls inside her shirt. And they very much wanted to be free.

The ensemble was made complete by a set of seven-million-inch silver sparkling stilettos.

Angie stood back and assessed her handiwork. "You're smokin' hot. It's perfect. What do you think?" Unable to wait for a response, she grabbed Verity by the shoulders and smiled proudly. "You're gorgeous. High tit!"

They bumped boobs again until one of Verity's popped out

of her bra.

"Let's go make Tattoo's balls cry!" Angie shouted.

They piled into an Uber, Verity nearly flashing her ass at the world as she climbed inside. This skirt was nothing like the ones she wore to work—more like one she'd wear to *work*. She was learning now that it wasn't super functional for sitting. Not that she planned to do much sitting at the bar. She would confront Hudson, give him hell for being so pissy about her asking questions, and maybe try to have a real conversation—though she wasn't exactly dressed or mentally prepared for that last part. She and Angie hadn't thought much past the hotness assault.

Surely Hudson wasn't a bad guy. And surely if he thought about it a little he could understand why she'd needed to perform a mini-inquisition. A hit of anger raced through her. He'd better not be lying. Because that she couldn't tolerate. She was finished with the part of her life that involved a liar.

Verity now knew for certain she was drunk and confused. But she would carry out this half-assed plan anyway, because that's what people did when they were drunk and making bad choices.

The Library Bar was packed when they arrived. Verity strut-wobbled inside, clutching Angie's arm for support. She knew why these horrible shoes had never been out of the box. They were a nightmare. *She* was a bit of a nightmare right now. Dressing a little outside her usual norm—well, a lot outside it—had felt empowering in the closet with Angie, but out and about, she worried she wouldn't seem appropriately serious about talking to Hudson. The hungry looks—and was that an ass grab?—from men in the crowded front section seemed to confirm this fear.

After a moment she spotted Hudson at the bar. Oh, God. He looked delicious. His beanie had been discarded on the bar beside him, and his hair stuck up in the back, like a little kid who'd been rushed out of bed in the morning and forgot to use a comb.

He wore a pair of low-slung jeans and a studded belt. His T-shirt hugged all the perfect muscles in his back and his slumped, defeated shoulders. He knocked back his drink and signaled the bartender for another. He thumb-typed something on his phone, then dropped it back on the bar.

Verity rooted around in her purse until she found her phone and checked Twitter.

**Hudson Fenn** @tatwhiteknight
That you'd believe that fuckhead over me says a lot.

He was still trying to Twitter fight.

She shoved her phone back in her purse and teetered over to him. Someone definitely tried to pinch her ass this time. She punched him in the dick, drunken ninja style.

Hudson didn't so much as glance at her when she sidled up beside him, getting right into his personal space. When he continued to ignore her, she employed her first tactic, words:

"I thought this might be an easier way to have our conversation."

Hudson looked up from his drink, his blue, slightly bloodshot eyes widening when he realized she was the one invading his bubble. His eyes slid from her face to her chest and then lower. His mouth dropped and suddenly he scanned the room, frantic. He brought his hands up, and moved them around, wax-on, wax-off style. It looked like an interpretive dance.

"Are you trolling for men?" He seemed incredulous, and pissed, and rather turned on.

"Maybe. You're the one Twitter fighting with me. I came to talk in person. I had the crappiest of mind-bendingly crappy days today. And when I dare to ask you to help me sort through things, you freak! What am I supposed to think? You're all—" She gestured to his appearance. "And secretive. And your dick is pierced!" *Shit.* That last part wasn't supposed to be spoken aloud.

"What?" Hudson pushed his stool back and stood.

He tried to put an arm around her, but she shoved it away. "You don't get to break up with me and then put your hands on me!"

"Break up with you?" He looked confused. And panicked. And angry.

"You yelled at me and pulled a Batman out my window!" Verity shouted. People were looking, and not just because her top was like a mirror and her skirt seriously needed more fabric.

"You're right. We do need to talk. In private." Hudson's jaw ticked. It was hot, like a super-spicy dried meat stick from 7-Eleven.

He held out his hand and waited for Verity to take it. When she hesitated, he leaned over to whisper to her. "Every guy in this entire bar is looking at you right now, and unless you want me perpetuate the stereotype you're so intent on assigning me by forcing me to commit mass murder, you'd better damn well come with me."

Verity wanted to be affronted by his order, not turned on, but he was so sexy and angry. He also clearly knew her well, which was a good sign, wasn't it? Or just a sign of thorough researching? The idea of mass murder over her was a little exciting, as well as terrifying, of course. Also, her judgment had disappeared, riding into the sunset on an alcohol-fueled emotional roller coaster. For one or more of those reasons, she allowed Hudson to guide her through the bar, shooting hate-glares at anyone who dared look at her. Which was everyone, thanks to her ridiculous skirt and batshit-crazy attitude.

They came to a set of stairs at the back of the bar, which Verity had never noticed before. A burly, bearded bouncer barred the way. He looked Verity over like she was a burger he'd consider eating.

Hudson snapped his fingers in his face. "Eyes over here."

Burly bouncer narrowed his squinty gaze.

"I need a VIP room. Now."

"This isn't that kind of place. There's a hotel down the street," Burly said with almost no inflection.

Hudson pulled out his wallet and flashed a pile of benjamins. Like, a legit pile. "She's not a goddamn hooker, she's my girlfriend."

When Burly glanced at Verity, Hudson snapped his fingers an inch from his face. "Do I need to speak to your manager? Look at her again, and you'll be out of a fucking job."

"Room Three." Burly took three bills from Hudson's ragey fingers and dropped a key in his hand.

That was a lot of money for a bike messenger to shell out so they could talk in private. Where had all the money came from?

Was the illegal sex doll trade truly that lucrative?

"I'll call for service when I want it." Hudson gestured for her to go ahead of him.

She held the railing tightly and teetered up the stairs.

Hudson muttered something behind her.

Three guys appeared at the landing, hesitating as Verity continued her perilous climb. At least Hudson was behind her to prevent her from falling all the way to the bottom. One of the guys made clicking sounds with his teeth as they approached.

"I will murder the fuck right out of you if you so much as breathe in her goddamn direction," Hudson growled.

The new death threats made Verity's lady parts swoon.

"Sorry, man," one of the guys muttered, rushing down the stairs.

"Verity! What are you doing?" Angie called from below on the other side of the bouncer. "I can see up your skirt! In hindsight, cheekies might have been the better option!"

Verity put her hands on her ass, and Hudson looked over his shoulder.

"We're going to talk," he called down.

"I'm out," Angie yelled in parting. "I still have to work tomorrow!"

Verity waved, but lost her focus as Hudson took another step up so his chest and then his stomach brushed against the back of her. "If you're going commando, I might lose my ever-loving shit."

Verity's knees wobbled, and not because of the insane shoes. She huffed indignantly and faux-stomped up the remaining stairs, carefully.

Verity had never been to a VIP room. She half expected it to have beds covered in plastic wrap for illicit fucking. Instead, Hudson ushered her into a low-lit room with a couch and two plush chairs. A table in the middle boasted fake candles and a chilled bottle of champagne. So this was what people with money to burn did on their nights out.

She turned to Hudson with her arms crossed under her breasts. He hung the Do Not Disturb sign on the door and closed it. As his eyes swept over her, anger and hunger seemed to fuse. Verity remembered what he'd done with all that hunger the last time they'd been together, and her vagina whimpered through the lips on her face.

But first they needed to clear the air.

"Why are you a bike messenger if you're an MIT graduate?" Verity asked. Might as well cut to the damn chase.

"Why are you dressed like… like…" Hudson gestured to her outfit.

Verity propped a hand on her hip. "Like what?" She dared him to offend her with his assessment.

"Like that."

Verity smoothed her hands down her hips, checking that her skirt was still R-rated and not X-rated. "It's my going-out outfit."

"Is it now?" Hudson took a step closer. He looked every bit as dangerous as she'd originally thought he was when he stole that cab. "Well, let me tell you something. Once we manage to sort this out, we'll either re-categorize that as a staying-in outfit, or I will burn it until it's nothing but a pile of ash."

"I paid good money for this. And now that I'm out of a job, I might need to start hooking, so you can't burn it."

"I'm thrilled that you're out of a job, and I'm sorry it took a sex doll to get you there. I know that had to have been a horrifying experience. I... um, I might have overreacted to your questions." Hudson looked intense, then his eyes darted to the floor.

Verity hugged herself, relieved, but looking for courage. "Tell me more, then. I need to hear it from your face that Larold Lay doesn't know you better than I do. And please don't lie to me."

Hudson jammed his hands in his pockets. "It's my uncle's company, but I don't work for him. He's my mom's brother, so I get along with him a lot better than I do other parts of my family. I know he takes pride in what he does and wouldn't betray his clients, but HoneyBee is his business. I stay out of it. And anyway, I'm not good at sharing stuff about myself. I just need you to trust me."

Verity scoffed. "Trust has to be earned. You can't get mad because I'm asking questions to look out for myself. If you'd stuck around to talk to me about it, I'm sure I would have believed you. But when you run off, it looks like one more thing you're hiding."

Hudson ripped off his beanie and ran a hand through his hair, making it look like a chaotic cornfield. He stepped into her personal space, popping it with hot, masculine aggression.

Verity was hopped up on booze and adrenaline, both of which made her want to get him naked and ride out her frustrations.

"Lay said the company hired an MIT grad to design realistic vaginas, and you're an MIT grad." He was so close, all she could manage was a whisper. "And you've performed many very thorough explorations of my vagina with both your tongue and your fingers. So, so thorough."

"And you think I did that so I could do what—make a Verity pocket pussy?"

"I—I don't know. I don't think so, but—"

His chest brushed her nipples. "You think a lowly bike messenger could design something as sophisticated as that? You think I could memorize every dip and curve of your pussy? That I'd know two fingers is tight and three makes you moan my name? That there's a tiny mole on your right pussy lip, and that your clit peeks out just a little when we get started and then swells like it's been stung by a bee when I lick you?"

Verity stifled a moan and clenched her hands at her sides, exhaling a harsh breath right in his face. It probably smelled like Fireball. Standing here now, Lay's accusations seemed ridiculous again. Her brain had just been scrambled before. It was kind of scrambled now. Instead of answering, she fisted Hudson's shirt and dragged his mouth to hers.

He remained frozen for a second before he responded. Then one hand went into her hair, and his tongue shot angrily into her mouth. The other hand went to the bottom of her skirt. It wasn't a far reach. Verity moaned. They were supposed to be arguing, not sword-fighting with their tongues. But God, she was so frustrated with the entire situation, and now she was horned up. They could argue with words later.

He grabbed a handful of her ass, and Verity pressed her hips into his, seeking the hard, pierced lump inside his jeans. He wrenched his mouth away from hers. "Why did you come here?"

"To tell you not to lie to me, and not to leave when we have things to discuss." She could feel the moisture in her eyes. She was due a good cry. Instead Verity said through several panted breaths, "And to give you a piece of my mind."

"A piece of your mind or a piece of your ass?" He smacked her bottom and she gasped, pushing on his chest. Hudson tightened his grip, using her ass cheek as an anchor. "Answer the question, Verity."

"A piece of my mind."

"Then why the hell did you wear this?"

"I don't know. Angie thought… So you'd see what you were missing. To make you mad."

"You mean so everyone else could see?"

His fingers dug into her skin, his pinkie finger getting close to her desperately hungry vagina. She flexed the muscles down there, as if it would draw him in.

"You ran away."

"You believed Lay."

"He designed a creepy sex doll of me! I'm a little weirded out!"

Hudson released her and held her at arm's length for a moment. Then he nodded. It was enough of an admission for her. Verity stumbled forward and hugged him.

Hudson dropped his mouth to hers like she was his last dinner before the Titanic sank. He shoved her skirt up over her hips. "If you ever wear this skirt anywhere but your apartment I'm going to take it out on your ass," he threatened.

"With your dick? Because I've never done that before, and I'm not sure it'll fit," Verity asked, her butt clenching at the thought.

"With my hand, Verity. Don't give me ideas."

They started tearing at each other's clothes. Well, Verity tore at Hudson's clothes. Hudson didn't have to do much other than find and flick open her bra to get her mostly naked. The skirt he left where it was. Her panties got caught on her ridiculous heels and hung there as he lifted her, wrapping her legs around his waist.

His pants halfway down his legs, he carried her awkwardly across the room to the couch. They dropped there, Verity under Hudson. She wondered, briefly, how many other asses had been pounded into these cushions.

Hudson shifted, his fingers slipping between her legs, and groaned. "Fuck, Honeybee, you're all wet for me."

Verity doubted he meant for it to rhyme, and she still wasn't sure how she felt about that nickname, but she couldn't argue. Their mutual frustration was horny-making. He rubbed frantically at her clit, then slipped two fingers inside her, pumping hard and fast. Verity grabbed his man stick and nudged his fingers out of the way. She wasn't interested in foreplay. All she wanted was pierced dick.

He pushed up on his arms so he could look at her. "Does me threatening mass murder turn you on?" He moved her hand and took hold of his cock. Verity looked down, watching his tattooed hand stroking slowly before he pulled a condom out of his back pocket and dressed his dick for business. He rubbed the pierced head around her clit in a circle.

Verity moaned rather than using words. She wasn't sure what it said about her that she kind of got off on that. And the sex in a semi-public place where other people had likely also fornicated didn't hurt either.

She lifted her hips and tried to get his dick closer to where she wanted it to make a home, but Hudson whacked her clit with it instead. "Answer the question and you can have my cock."

"You threatening to murder people gets me hot, and just you

in general, and you being angry and threatening those guys—and you being a bike messenger-MIT graduate from the craziest family ever also makes me irrationally hot. Now will you fuck me? Please."

Hudson cocked a sexy brow and smirked. But it wasn't an amused smirk, it was a dark one. He sat back on his knees, picked her up, and flipped her over so she was ass up, taking care to avoid the spikes of her shoes. He rearranged her to hold on to the back of the couch. She looked over her shoulder, gasping as he slapped her clit with the head of his cock. "You asked for it, so get ready, Verity."

She gripped the horrible burgundy velour and groaned when he pushed into her with one swift, hard thrust. "Oh God, it's pierced cock magic!" she cried.

Hudson slapped her ass like they were in one of those terrible music videos, and then he made good on the fucking. He pounded her until the hashtag was branded on her pussy. Leaning over her, he brought his lips to her ear, biting the lobe. "I'm so fucking mad at you right now."

"I know," she moaned. "I'm mad at you, too." She slapped at his thigh and grabbed his hair, trying to secure their mouths together despite the vigorous pounding. "But your prick is a miracle."

It wasn't possible to kiss and angry-fuck without potentially biting each other's tongues off. So Verity gave up on the kissing and held on as the couch inched its way from the center of the room to the wall.

"You better not come before me," she threatened. It was the worst threat, because she had no recourse other than possibly withholding her vagina from him, which was unlikely, considering how much she loved his dick.

Hudson reached between her legs and started rubbing like he was trying to light her clit on fire. Verity came so hard she almost bit a hole in the couch. Hudson kept up the driving thrusts until his rhythm faltered and broke.

He groaned into the side of her neck and collapsed on top of her. "I'm still mad at you."

"Me too. But that helped a little."

Hudson snorted and pushed off of her. He pulled his jeans up and tucked himself away. Verity's panties were stuck to the bottom of her shoe. She wasn't all that interested in putting them back on, but did so anyway, needing the limited vag shield they provided. Sequins had fallen off her shirt and sprinkled the couch, making it look like a burgundy night sky. She struggled to refasten her bra. When Hudson was fully dressed, he helped put her back together.

"We still need to talk."

"I know." Verity tried to pull her skirt down, but it was useless.

Hudson regarded her for a long moment. "Come on, let's get out of here. He grabbed the bottle of champagne and her hand, pulling her off the couch.

Verity was still orgasm-uncoordinated and stumbled into him. Now that the sex was over, she felt a little dirty. A thousand asses had sat on that couch before her face was in the cushions. Hudson opened the door and stepped out into the hall.

"I can't go back through the bar," Verity protested. "People will know we had sex, and they'll think I'm actually a hooker."

"Now you admit this outfit is nuts?"

"You sexed me hard, of course I can admit it now. Just like

you can admit you kind of like it when I look slutty."
He nodded. "We'll go out the back way."
"There's a back way?"
"There's always a back way." He winked.
She followed Hudson the opposite way down the hall. They came to a stairwell, and Verity teetered down three flights, holding onto the railing like it was a cock made of gold. Her heels were going in the garbage tomorrow.
They burst out the back entrance into a parking lot. "Are we getting a cab?"
"We'll take my ride."
"I can't double on a bike, Hudson."
He produced a set of keys from his pocket. Somewhere in the lot, a car chirped and lights flashed. Taking his offered hand, Verity stumble-walked across the uneven pavement. When they reached the car, she stopped and shot a wary glance at Hudson.
"Did you steal this?"
He raised a brow. "Nope."
"Is it a rental?"
"Nope again. Remember what they say about appearances." Hudson opened the door of the grey Audi R8.
Verity slipped into the passenger seat of the car that cost more than any she'd ever been in before. "If you tell me that room I can't go into at your place is a Red Room of Pain, we're going to need to stop to buy lube and some Fifty Shades wine."

**Verity Michaels** @VerityPics03
VIP room couches are steam-cleaned daily, right?
#CelebrityJizz #AssToMouth #SilkwoodShower

**Hudson Fenn** @tatwhiteknight
VIP — Very Impatient Pussy. #ThatWasNotARealSkirt

**Verity Michaels** @VerityPics03
Why don't you just STFU and drive? #StillMad

**Hudson Fenn** @tatwhiteknight
#MadderThanYou

**Verity Michaels** @VerityPics03
You're a #TwitterWhiner #LastWord

# Chapter 20

### Miracle Prick
### S.M. Lumetta

Verity squirmed in the Audi's passenger seat. "Don't look at me like that, Tattoo," she warned.

He almost grinned.

"Are you okay to drive? You've been drinking for a while." Verity tried to squint, but between her own pre-stalking, rage-drinking and the VIP pounding she'd taken, her physical responses were a bit disconnected. Hudson didn't seem impaired, so she just prayed they wouldn't get in an accident. She didn't want anyone else, let alone cops and EMTs, to see her in this getup.

"I'm fine," he assured her. "I was pacing myself, despite what the tweets said. Plus I think I burned off anything I drank the second I saw you in that outfit." He revved the engine.

"All the booze went to your dick?" *Put a cork in it, Verity.*

He rolled his eyes and peeled out.

"Oh, Christ, do you even have a license?" she asked. "You

realize I'm still kinda drunk, don't you?"

"I would never have guessed," he said. "My miracle prick didn't sober you up?"

The thought of his miracle prick so close made her quiet. Just as she was ready to point out helpfully that he'd driven past his building, he turned the corner and pulled into an underground garage. The door shut behind them.

"Is the torture chamber in the basement? Or is it just cages?" she asked, noticing the pounding headache that had developed during the drive. *Ugh, more pounding. Wrong kind.* "Will I be chained when you question me?"

He shook his head when she looked over at him. "Would you like to be?" he asked, but got out of the car without waiting for an answer.

She scrambled out and followed him to the elevator. "It'd either be cool or terrifying to have sex in here," she mused as they ascended. Then she realized she'd spoken aloud.

Hudson tried unsuccessfully to smother a smirk. "Pretty awesome, I'd say."

"I don't want to know," she grumbled. Jealousy made her feel whore-ier.

"I *mean*," he said, "that I *think* it would be. We can add that to the list of fun projects for later."

She vowed not to speak for the rest of the ride up to his floor, and when they entered his too-nice-for-a-bike-messenger place for a second time, she tried to reserve judgment. She needed an actual tour this time.

"You want something to drink?" Hudson asked. "As in water? Or coffee?"

They turned into a wide galley kitchen. She chose water and

tried to crane her neck around the corner. Hudson pulled out a couple of pint glasses, filled them, and handed one to her.

She eyed him. "So now what?"

"Now I'm going to give you a shirt or something to put on, because I cannot talk seriously with your pussy glaring at me."

"She's not glaring," Verity offered. "She's dazed. Decent sex and all." No amount of adjusting could get her skirt to lay right after they'd bunched it up on the VIP couch.

"Decent?" He raised an eyebrow at her in challenge.

"Fine, mind-blowing," she said with an eye roll.

One corner of his mouth lifted as he turned and walked away. "I'll get you that shirt."

She yanked her tiny skirt down over her butt as best she could and kicked off her shoes to wander farther inside. The apartment was shockingly well-decorated in an industrial man-chic kind of style. She touched the forbidden doorknob. It wasn't locked, so she took a deep breath and opened the door. In the middle of a medium-sized bedroom, a vintage dentist's chair had been screwed to the floor. Along the wall across from it stood an old medical cabinet and a makeshift drafting table. Along the other wall sat a seriously comfortable-looking sofa. She saw nothing that looked like doll-making materials. But still, this was not a room that came standard in anyone's house.

"What the hell?" she called. "Do you run some kind of fucked-up medical practice? Black-market organ removal? Bizarre, illegal surgical experiments?"

Hudson exhaled as he came up behind her and thrust a well-worn concert tee into her hand. "Here, put this on."

Verity pulled it over her head, grateful that it fell three inches past the hem of her skirt.

"Let's sit down, okay?" Hudson urged. He walked over to the massive, badass couch and settled in.

Verity remained standing. "Do you add some spider webs and fake blood for Halloween? Are you part of a haunted house tour?"

The look on his face told her he was not going to answer. Again.

Verity walked over to the dentist chair and plopped herself in it.

"How about you answer my question?"

He curled his body forward slowly enough that she was distracted by the way the muscles in his arms bulged and flexed as he pushed off.

"I haven't lied to you, Verity," he said.

"So I'm supposed to trust you completely because you have a miraculously amazing pierced dick?"

"No. You should believe me because you've seen what kind of person I am. I've told you things I hadn't shared with anyone. You should believe me because I've been fighting for this relationship with you."

"Right now I'm sitting in a room that makes no sense, and you don't see why that bothers me? Tell me about it," she urged. "Please. Show me that you trust me too. What's the deal with this chair?" she asked, running her hands over its wide arms.

"I'm not sure I should disclose that information," he said, oddly but intentionally formal. He seemed to be swallowing the words he wished he could say. "I trust you," he added. "But this room and what happens here is not just about me."

She thought for a moment, wondering what she was missing. Then she decided maybe the best way to be worthy of Hudson's trust was to deem him worthy of hers. "In addition to being freaked out today by meeting a latex version of myself, let me try to explain why, in general, secrets can often seem like lies to me," she began.

And then she told him the story she'd never dared tell anyone, maybe even herself: how her mother's version of being an artist was more like drinking a lot and never coming home, how gallery shows and mingling had taken precedence over her husband and daughter, and how saying one thing and doing the opposite had become the standard for Verity's mother and her child.

"I've vowed never to let myself be hurt like that again," Verity finally said. "I need to know the truth. I can't just accept what you tell me because that didn't work out well for me when I was growing up."

"Okay, I get it." Hudson took a deep breath. "What do you want to know?"

"What happens here? Why can't you tell me?" Verity crossed her arms over his concert T-shirt.

He gave her a look that clearly weighed and measured their entire relationship and everything she'd just told him before sighing. "Remember when I told you about Spring Felt? My mom's tattoo artist who became my tattoo artist?" He lifted an eyebrow.

Verity nodded.

"Well, she retired a few years ago, but before that I apprenticed with her, learned from her. Turns out I'm pretty good at more than *drawing* tattoos. So when she was done, she directed her clients to me." He bit his thumb.

"You give people tattoos? Okay. I guess that's what this chair is for. But what's the big deal? Why keep that a secret?"

"Well, Spring had quite a reputation, and many of her clients—now my clients—are people you've heard of, people you'd recognize. People who value their privacy and don't want media coverage of the fact that they're getting a tattoo." He paused meaningfully, and Verity felt her eyes widen as understanding dawned on her.

"You're a tattoo artist to the stars! You're smokin' and jokin' and pokin' the best and the brightest with needles. I *knew* you had a deviant streak," she giggled. "I'm just so glad it's not criminal!"

"Yeah, I'm super deviant," he said with a snort. "Tattooing someone is about trust—holding their trust and keeping your word. Sometimes there's also a non-disclosure agreement involved. All very kinky and scandalous. It's actually a big pain in the ass sometimes—I get calls at odd hours, last-minute requests, huge egos to manage, and a really weird work schedule, which is why I keep it to only a select group of clients."

"Okay!" Verity nodded. "And you clearly make good money. So why do you work as a bike messenger? For kicks?"

"Basically. I have the time, and I get to ride around the city, run into all sorts of only-in-New-York situations, meet people—among them a stunningly gorgeous yet insane country girl who thinks I'm a deviant—and I get my inspiration. Plus, it pisses off my dad. I love delivering to his building so I can demonstrate to all of them what a huge failure I am."

"*That* is a little deviant," Verity noted. "And I like it."

Hudson smiled big, looking hugely relieved. "Spring gave me an amazing gift, and I never want to let her down. If word got out about my client list, my whole business—her whole legacy—would collapse. So that's why I don't share this part of myself with anyone. Well, until now."

For some reason, Verity felt herself blushing. She looked at the floor. "I didn't *really* think you were a deviant."

"You practically came when you thought I would kill people over that outfit you wore."

"You have to know that's not really what turned me on. I liked that you were possessive of me," she admitted. She took in a quick breath and met his stunned eyes. "I...I really liked that you seemed to want me for yourself."

"I do." His eyes were wide and clear. She saw something in them that sent shivers through her entire body. "Fuck, Verity."

She pulled herself out of the chair and swooned a bit. "Fuck you, Fireball," she mumbled.

He laughed. "You drank Fireball? That's some shit whiskey, baby."

At the thought of all that had accompanied the Fireball, Verity felt a little green. But not even the mother hangover she knew was coming could mar her happiness. Trust was kind of an amazing thing, and Hudson seemed to be the king of it.

She sighed into a smile. "Do you mind if I grab a quick shower?" When his smile went from congenial to lustful she put up a hand. "It's going to be medically thorough, so maybe I can get it alone."

Hudson nodded like the gentleman she believed he was. "I'll get you clothes to change into."

She followed him to his bedroom where he provided her with yet another concert tee and a pair of boxer briefs, then directed her into his shower.

Twenty minutes later, feeling steam-cleaned with the pink skin to prove it, Verity found Hudson unlocking a set of glass French doors at the back of the kitchen. As he entered, she heard a chorus of sweet meows. She walked around the island to see a herd of kitties rubbing on his legs.

"Um...you really like pussy, huh?" she said.

He smiled and winked. "I foster for a few rescues and shuttle them around to the cat cafes in the Village so they can get adopted."

"Seriously? Your lifestyle affords such luxuries!" Verity cocked a hip out to the side, enjoying the new, lighter mood.

He smiled, and it was like sunshine. She returned her attention to the mass of cats at their feet. After a moment she saw extra toes and *squee*d.

"Omigod! He's a Hemingway kitty—um, a polydactyl."

"Yep." Hudson nodded. "That's Hunter. And the rest are Tiger, Lola, and Killer."

Verity snickered. "Killer? Which one?"

Hudson pointed to the smallest, a brown tabby with one eye missing.

"Of course he is."

"She," he said, and they locked eyes. "I took her in the day after I met you."

She stared at her tattooed bad boy-good guy for a moment. Lifting up onto her toes, she kissed him lightly.

"You should keep her," she said.

He dropped Killer to the floor, where she mewed and began rolling and batting with the others at their feet. "I'd like to," he said, pulling Verity close. "Think she'd like that?"

"Yep. I'm sure of it," she said.

**Verity Michaels** @VerityPics03
My boyfriend loves the pussy. #CatCondo #Weirdo <3

**Hudson Fenn** @tatwhiteknight
My girlfriend loves that I love the pussy. #Killer Did you just <3 me?

**Verity Michaels** @VerityPics03
Can't tweet anymore. Oral afterglow. #ChangingThisAcct2NSFW <3 <3

**Hudson Fenn** @tatwhiteknight
Put the phone down, woman. I'm not done with you. #VeryNSFW <3 <3 <3

# Chapter 21

### Slick Glass
### Nina Bocci/ Debra Anastasia

Even in a sleepy fog, Verity enjoyed the soft kisses Hudson peppered across her shoulder and neck. His rough, sandpaper tongue darted out to kiss her chin while his fuzzy beard tickled her nose. *Wait, what?*

She cracked her eyes open, took a moment to thank the heavens she didn't feel as awful as she deserved to after last night's ridiculous drinking, and came face to face with Killer, who sat on her chest meowing. Embarrassed, she reached over for Hudson, but his side of the bed was empty—still warm though, so she scooped up the kitten and padded across the chilly floor in search of him.

The shower was running, steam pouring from beneath the door. "Sorry, Killer. You're not going to like what goes down in here," she whispered. She kissed the cat on top of its soft head before setting her down on a side table with an antique microscope on it.

Verity cracked the door and slipped inside. The room was stifling, billowing with steam that caressed and warmed her skin.

Watching Hudson's figure in the steamy shower, she thought back over last night—the whole of last night, not just the sex parts, although *damn*. Things felt different now. Hudson was much less a mystery to her, and he'd been willing to learn her secrets too. Each time they'd talked had revealed another piece of her heart to him, and the weight of his trust in her, his belief in her, felt luxuriously wonderful.

Her nipples tightened as she watched the silhouette of his body beneath the shower heads. What she wouldn't give to be a droplet of water sluicing between the dips and valleys of his body, sliding over the colorful landscape that was his skin.

"You staring at me has raised the heat in here by twenty degrees," Hudson called over the water. One of his hands slapped the glass high above his head and slid down. She watched with fascination as the steam filled in the clear spot in a matter of moments. He did it again, this time with both hands. He slid them against the slick, steamed-up glass until they exposed his face.

His wicked smile was covered by the steam as he spoke. "I need some help," he said, pushing forward enough that the piercing on his hard cock left its own trail along the glass.

Without a second thought, she stalked toward the shower and stepped inside. Verity felt empowered, brazen, more sexually alive than she'd ever been in her life. She and Hudson truly were something together.

Silently, he pulled her under the water warm from the rain shower overhead. He pushed her hair back, kissing along her forehead, across her temples, and over her cheeks while his hands took the stretched-out sides of the shirt she wore and pulled them, making the gaping arm holes even larger.

It shouldn't have been sexy; what he was doing should have looked ridiculous, but Verity watched with rapt attention as he maneuvered the arm holes across her chest, framing her breasts with the now-transparent white fabric.

He kneeled before her on the tiles, gripping the shirt with one hand to keep it between her breasts. "I like them like this," he murmured before taking a nipple in his mouth.

When her knees wobbled, he spun her so she could lean back against the shower glass for support. She imagined what someone walking in might see: her skin flush against the slick glass, no steam covering her up, her bare ass pressed against it.

She gasped as Hudson pulled as much of her breast into his mouth as he could. She took the shirt from his hand and ripped it, fully exposing herself to his ravaging mouth.

"Someone is feisty this morning," he said as he sat back on his haunches.

He stroked his cock once before he went to his knees and laid it hard and thick against the tile, the silver at the tip sparkling in the water.

Verity had a war raging within her. She wanted nothing more than to grip his head and pull his tongue onto her clit. Or throw him down onto the tile and ride his face until she came. Another bit of her tried to smother the surge of energy and just relish Hudson's wickedness—see where he took this.

While she was overthinking things, he spread her out before him with soft fingers.

"Mmm," he whispered, the words almost drowned out by the

water surrounding them.

Her head thudded against the glass, the vibration shooting up her back. She looked around the shower, trying to find something, anything to focus on besides Hudson rubbing his nose against her, teasing. His tongue followed and then the second-most beloved piercing lit her up from the inside out, slowly and methodically destroying her.

Her entire body shook, and she thought she might implode from the want coursing through her. Everything was more intense now.

When his tongue connected with her clit again, she nearly cried in relief. He moaned, and the vibration set her off quickly.

"Again," he coaxed, using one hand to keep her open and the other to tease at her entrance. With one finger inside, he curled it upward until her body pitched forward, slumping against him for support.

"Hudson, no more," she begged weakly, but he paid her pleas no mind. Instead he added another finger, filling her.

"More..." He spoke against her, adding a third.

That was when she broke, again—thrashing against the glass, against him.

Looking pleased with himself, he unfurled from his position on the tile and stretched his arms above his head.

"Okay?" he asked, smiling down at her. "I have something else for you."

Though sated and a bit jelly-like, she perked up when his cock brushed against her.

"I'm not sure I'll be of any use," she said, trying to will movement into her melted bones.

Hudson moved to the faucets, turned a few knobs, and before

she knew it, water sprayed out of side jets directly onto her.

He slunk back to her and moved his hands to her waist. Lifting her easily, he pinned her to the glass. The water swept past them like speeding traffic, heating up the shower even more.

"You don't have to do anything. I got this," he told her. And with that promise, he slipped inside. He buried his head near her neck and began to move.

"Faster," she moaned, pulling at his hair. She kissed him hungrily, gripping and clutching his slick back.

"No, like this," he grunted, keeping his agonizing pace.

It felt like one long, drawn-out, blinding orgasm that built from the tips of her hair to the red paint on her toes. Her body sang, hummed along with the music of the water that splashed around them.

"Huds—fuck me, fuck," she moaned.

He finally picked up speed, his knuckles knocking against the glass as he came.

He stayed inside her for a moment or ten. She wasn't sure of anything other than her singular focus on the bright silver rain showerhead above them.

"I can't get enough of you," he said, lowering her slowly to the tile. He led her to the wide teak bench to sit.

As Hudson pushed another few buttons and spun knobs, the water stopped and the steam picked up, swelling in the shower like a rising ghost. "This will keep us warm until we can—"

"—function?" she finished, curling up at his side.

"That's a great way of putting it." Hudson pulled her close and kissed the top of her wet head.

"You have a great way of putting it too." Verity bit her lip when he growled and pulled her onto his lap, where she straddled him. They spent some time hugging like this, the steam making the whole thing seem like a dream.

"So what now, Verity Michaels? What would you like to do with your day? With your life?"

She took in his dimples and white teeth as he smiled at her before hitting the back of his front teeth gently with the tongue piercing.

"I don't know. My dad would probably find me a couple hundred more interviews as soon as I tell him I'm out of a job."

"He doesn't know yet?"

"No. There's a lot of explaining that will have to go along with that, and I like to sandwich bad news in between two slices of good news." She trailed her fingers over Hudson's collarbone, thinking about how her father would react to the silent rebellion on his skin.

"Am I bad news, baby?"

He'd read her mind.

She squeezed her eyes shut against all the sexual innuendoes she wanted to make. "For me you're not," she said when she'd recovered. "You're the best news. For Dad? Well, he will need to get to know you. He judges first, but he does come around. At least that's my hope. I actually think you guys would get along great."

"Thanks for thinking that." He rested his hands on her hips.

"It's true. I can't think of a single person that matters to me who wouldn't be crazy about you as soon as they got to know you. You're a chameleon—you can be fancy and rich or riding a bike or inking a tattoo. I'm proud of who you are." She touched his forehead and traced his sharp cheekbone down to his stubble-lined jaw.

"And how I look?"

She saw a hint of insecurity before he put his gaze on her lips instead of her eyes.

She put one hand on either side of his gorgeous face. "You're a masterpiece. A treasure. And the inside is as beautiful as the outside." She kissed the tip of his nose as she watched him blush under her fingers.

This man—who'd helped his mother until she couldn't fight anymore, this person who refused to conform to his father's will—he was exceptional. And he needed this adoration. Not just the physical appreciation, but to know the way her heart felt when she saw him, the way she felt safe when he smiled at her.

She kissed him with those thoughts soaring in her mind. She hoped he could taste them a little.

After breakfast, they cuddled up on Hudson's couch in sweats. They'd resolved to let the question of Verity's future go unanswered for a while longer and just be. Hudson thought the "just being" phase might even take a few days—a week tops. But presented with the bounty of Netflix, neither of them could seem to decide on something to watch.

The trailer for a documentary about sex robots popped up,

and Verity felt it was a sign. She had to bring up something still bothering her.

"You know, the thought of Larold 'using' the rubber Verity makes me squeamish—even if it doesn't actually have my face." She pulled her legs up under her.

Hudson narrowed his eyes. "I could beat the ever-living shit out of him."

"You could. And I could watch." Verity let herself picture that and felt a satisfied smile pull at her lips. But then she shook her head. "I love when you're violent Hudson, but I really think he's weird, not dangerous. I mean, I guess if you left him in the pool toy aisle..."

She and Hudson made matching faces of revulsion before she continued. "He did say he was sorry, and he realized it was a mistake. I think he'll let me have it if I ask. I get the sense that he's really a broken guy. What leads a man to feel comfortable with dolls instead of a real person? He has lovers, and then has to create them again. It's almost like he makes dolls out of the women so he doesn't have to be involved with a human long-term. That's some serious baggage. And up until me, all the girls knew about it, agreed to it. But anyway, I kind of wish I had the doll and maybe his promise to not do it again."

Hudson lifted an eyebrow and picked up her phone from the coffee table. "May I?"

Verity shrugged, puzzled. "Sure."

He spoke to her phone's artificial intelligence. "Hey, can you dial Larold Lay at SalesExportt.com?"

"Dialing Larold Lay."

Verity covered her mouth with both hands.

Hudson cleared his throat as the call connected. "Yes, thank you, Marge. I need to speak with a Mr. Larold Lay? This is Hastens Furburger. I'm representing Ms. Verity Michaels in a lawsuit against your boss. Can you put me through to him?"

Verity mouthed, *Furburger???* before clamping her hands over her mouth to keep from laughing.

Hudson tipped a pretend hat at her and pulled her legs onto his lap.

"What are you doing?" she asked after Marge had put him on hold.

"I'm getting you that doll. You don't need to feel squeamish because of a guy's sexual desires, whether he's dangerous or not." Hudson gave her knee a reassuring squeeze before paying attention to her phone again. "Yes. Am I speaking with Larold Lay of SalesExportt.com?" He drummed on her knee with his fingertips.

He listened for a moment, and although Verity could hear the tone of Larold's voice, she couldn't make out his words.

"It's come to my attention that you have a rubberized likeness of my client, Verity S. Michaels, in your private corporate bathroom?"

After a moment Hudson's jaw clenched, and Verity heard a few words that indicated why.

"*Personal property... time investment... customized to my genitals.*"

That last one made Verity a little nauseated.

Hudson interrupted. "Know that this conversation is being recorded, Lay. The lawsuit I can file right now will implement a restraining order against you, protecting every inanimate object with an ethylene base from you for the rest of your natural born years."

Verity gave Hudson a perplexed look, and he shrugged and pantomimed whacking off.

She giggled again.

Hudson mouthed, *Got him!*

"Okay, can you then please send my client the doll in her likeness and agree right here on this recording that you will never create another sex doll without the woman in question's consent? Yes? Good. Then I'll forget this restraining order and perhaps persuade my client that a lawsuit won't be necessary…"

After Hudson ended the call, he turned to Verity and smiled. "He's going to send the doll via an overnight courier to this address. Is that okay? If you really want to sue him for harassment, I can help you."

Verity loved the look of determination in Hudson's face. "Thanks. A lot. I think I'll leave that option alone for a while. As long as we can track him to make sure he never does this again, I think it will be okay. Angie is pretty invested in her job there, and I think Lay is scared of her. He doesn't hit on her, so I'd like to not upend her life."

Hudson held out his arms, and she adjusted so she could put her head on his chest.

"First you steal a taxi, then we break into the Conservatory Garden. Now you've impersonated a lawyer. You are the trickiest white knight in the business."

"Anything for you, baby." Hudson put his chin on top of her head, and her heart did that warming up thing again.

The next day was festive, yet moderately terrifying, as it heralded the triumphant return of the faceless latex Verity doll. Larold had indeed sent it to Hudson's overnight, but Hudson had gone to work by the time the delivery came mid-morning. The box was so big and heavy, at least compared to all the other doll-parts boxes, that Verity worried Larold had mailed himself to her or something crazy. She called Hudson right away, and he instructed her not to touch it. Verity found a baseball bat in one of Hudson's closets and sat with it at the ready until he returned.

When he arrived, he kicked the box a time or two before opening it with a knife from the kitchen. It contained no human bodies, but latex Verity came in her own carrying case with her name embroidered on it. The sheer number of packing peanuts surrounding the deflated, carefully folded carcass would have kept a Fabergé egg safe on a cross-country journey by army tank. A very formal sheaf of documents included a wedding certificate Lay had made for the doll and himself and five pages of instructions outlining the care and handling of latex, faceless Verity.

Hudson read the whole thing over her shoulder before muttering, "Dude's got issues. That guy's issues have issues."

Verity shuffled through the last of the paperwork to find a generous personal check from Lay made out to the real Verity. An attached note explained that it was to fund the completion of the doll's face, as well as provide an outfit allowance and money to take the doll on the Hawaiian vacation he'd promised her.

"How would he even get the doll on a plane?" Verity asked, her mortification and Lay's latex love obsession reaching brain-melting levels.

"In a suitcase?" Hudson suggested. "Perhaps she travels in

her snazzy case there."

Verity could imagine her rubbery self dressed in a bikini, lying on a beach in Hawaii while Lay pretended she was actually real. That would haunt her dreams for the rest of her life. No way in hell would she use Lay's pervy fantasy money.

But before she could tear up the check, Hudson snatched it away. "Sweetness, this is what we're calling your severance package. You are cashing that shit."

Verity considered that for a moment, and realized he was right. Never look a gift horse in the mouth. Never look too closely at Larold Lay's anything.

"Okay, but we need to get rid of this." She gestured to the folded faceless effigy. "It's creepy, and I don't think I'll be able to sleep with it in my apartment. I keep imagining her coming to life to murder me and take over my identity."

"Wow. The things that happen in your head are wild." Hudson shook his head, but promised to take care of it. After a few phone calls, he'd managed to make arrangements to dispose of the latex body.

Verity invited Angie to join them for the doll's afterhours burial in the Conservatory Garden that night.

Just after sunset, Hudson's maintenance contact let them into the Garden grounds and directed them to an area being actively planted where the soil was loose. It was rather sexy to watch Hudson work a shovel in the semi-darkness of the security lights as he dug a hole for the nightmare that was rubber-doll Verity. At the end, she and Angie tossed a few flowers on the carrying case before he covered it with soil.

"Here lies faceless, rubber Verity," Hudson intoned. "May she find peace under the marigolds come spring."

Angie stifled a laugh. "Can we go get a drink now?"

Verity smiled as she felt her peace of mind return. This mafia-style burial of a sex doll would no doubt be a tale she and Hudson told while tits deep in the hot tub at an Ocala retirement park 40 years from now. It had been just a little criminal and a whole lot perfect. And this time, they left the Garden without being chased.

🐦

**Verity Michaels** @VerityPics03
Ever feel like you're burying the past behind you? #NoMoreRubberEver

🐦

**Hudson Fenn** @tatwhiteknight
The real thing is 100% better. #RealSkin #ThatSoundsWorse

# Chapter 22

## Happiest Vagina
## Leisa Rayven

On Friday morning, Verity awoke feeling deliciously lazy and snuggled further into Hudson's pillows as her coma-like post-sex slumber lifted. He'd convinced her to take a few days for herself before diving right into the job search, and *damn* if he wasn't a wise man. Nearly a week of self-indulgence had been heavenly. She'd reacquainted herself with her camera, explored the city with her favorite bike messenger, and even gotten to see Hudson the tattoo artist in action one night when a client came over.

This one hadn't been overly paranoid, so as long as she didn't talk and didn't stare, Verity was allowed to hang out with them while the work was done. Why anyone would want such a filthy word permanently printed on his lower back, Verity wasn't sure, but this guy always wore suits on TV, so maybe he figured it didn't matter. Rather than cursing through the pain, he'd cracked jokes, so Verity had felt like she was on the set of his show, without having to stay up quite so late.

Her smile faded as she rolled over and found nothing but cold sheets. Hudson was MIA, and it seemed he'd been gone a while. Her smile faded further as she reminded herself she was officially jobless, and today was the day to begin dealing with that. Manhattan was expensive, and even though Lay's "severance" was substantial, it would only keep the wolf from her door for so long. She reluctantly resigned herself to leaving her cocoon to deal with the messy reality of her life.

She threw off the covers and grabbed one of Hudson's crumpled T-shirts off the floor. When she pulled it over her head, a burst of his scent filled her nose, and her determination to find him and drag him back to bed intensified. Her messy life could wait a little longer.

She padded around the house, stopping at the room off the kitchen to peek for him. Hudson wasn't there, but his crew of cats was, including two still sleeping, wrapped around each other like yin and yang.

Verity smiled. "Morning, Killer." She stroked the cat's back, and the brown kitten purred so loudly the vibration tickled Verity's hand.

"Yeah, such a badass."

Killer rolled over to expose her tummy.

"Where's your dad, honey?"

More purring.

"Oh, he's off being a smoking-hot sex god? Yeah, well, duh. Tell me something I don't know." Verity added a bit more kitty love before resuming her search.

"Hudson?" she called, stepping back into the kitchen.

Silence greeted her. She stopped in the bathroom on her way

back down the hall. He wasn't there, but he had been. His scent hung in the air, and the shower had recently been used. Without her.

*Not cool, Tattoo. Not cool at all.*

She padded out into the empty dining room. Hudson wasn't there either, but on the table was a plate of fresh pastries, a grande Starbucks cup, and a note.

*Morning, Honeybee.*

The sight of her nickname in print stopped her for a moment. But she'd decided to own it, she reminded herself. Larold Lay would not be ruining a perfectly sweet nickname for her. She returned to reading.

*Sorry I had to bail. Have some packages to deliver today. Would have woken you, but two things prevented me. First of all, you look like a fucking angel when you sleep. Did you know that? I sat there for a while and just watched you, all messy hair and swollen lips. Anyone seeing you like that would never guess what a filthy perv you are in the bedroom.*

*Secondly, I knew that if I woke you, and you looked at me with those "please fuck me" eyes of yours, neither of us would get out of this apartment today, and that couldn't happen. My dick had other ideas, but he's not the boss of me.*

*Well, maybe he convinced me to pull the sheet down so I could stare at your rack like a creeper for a minute, but that's where I drew the line. At least he allowed me to drag myself away from you and go about my day. He's such a fucking dicktator. (See what I did there? Handsome and hilarious with a cock that just won't quit? No wonder you can't get enough of me.)*

At this point, Hudson had drawn a cartoon portrait of himself with two thumbs up and a shit-eating grin. He'd even made an attempt at capturing his tattoos. Verity laughed, startling the cats now peering at her through the French doors.

"You adorable idiot," she muttered to the note, and then kept reading.

*Anyway, I'll call you later. Not sure when. Feel free to hang out at my place if you like. You can watch TV. Eat my food. Rub your boobs on all my underwear. Whatever. Oh, but don't look in the bottom drawer of my dresser. That shit is private.*
*I'm serious.*
*X Hud*

Verity smiled down at the note. She had fallen hard for this guy, and there wasn't a damn thing she could do about it.
Thank God.
With a contented sigh, Verity picked up a pastry and took a huge bite. She ended up devouring three of the things as she drained the entire lukewarm cup of coffee. When she'd finished, she let out a huge belch.
The cats silently judged her.
"What?" she asked. "Like you've never had a sex marathon with a hottie in an alley and then binged on kibble. Please."
After clearing up the kitchen, Verity proceeded to have a scavenger hunt around Hudson's bedroom to find all her clothing. She eventually located everything except her

underpants, and for the life of her, she couldn't remember where they'd ended up. They'd been watching a movie last night before they'd turned to other activities, so she thought they might be on the couch, but nope. Deciding not to waste any more time, she gave up and went to shower.

She was preparing to head home when she remembered Hudson's note. Smiling to herself, she went back into the bedroom and opened the bottom drawer of his dresser. Inside sat a piece of paper with his messy handwriting on it.

*Honeybee! What the fuck? I told you this shit was private.*
*Close the drawer and walk away.*
*Now.*
*Don't make me ask you twice.*

"Pfft. Way to get me to absolutely *not* do that," she muttered.

She took the note out, along with the hastily folded T-shirt it sat on. Below it was another note.

*Woman, you are on dangerous ground now. I'm warning you, go no farther or face the consequences. That dentist's chair? I have restraints fitted to it. They're leather and unbreakable, and if you don't want to find out how uncomfortable they can be, leave.*
*Immediately.*
*I'm serious.*

Again she removed the note, along with a pair of grey sweats. Below, she found another note.

*You have a death wish, lady, don't you? I wish I'd known about this earlier. So, I'm going to mark you down for a round of severe discipline when I see you next. Where do you stand on ball-gags? Floggers? Anal beads? Yay or nay?*

Verity laughed and kept going. This time, below the note was a giant plastic bag of Star Wars action figures. She smirked in triumph. *Oh, Hudson. Really?* He'd led her to his hidden Nerdvana.

There was a message scribbled on the front of the bag:

*Okay, fine. So I figured you should know this about me as well: I have a serious thing for Star Wars. And yes, I even own a Jar Jar. Shut up. I'm a little OCD. When I get home, you can dress up like Princess Leia, if you'd like. Or I'll tattoo a detective badge on you to commemorate your excellent sleuthing. Now, get out of here.*

Verity giggled like a fool as she examined Hudson's collection. Man, there were a *lot* of them. At least fifty or sixty. So her ultra-male, hot-as-Hades, tattooed piece of man meat was also a total *Star Wars* geek? Dear God, why did that make him even more attractive? It didn't make sense.

She was about to put everything back into the drawer when she noticed another piece of paper poking out from under a gym towel.

*Seriously? There's more?*

She pulled out the towel, and yep. Another note.

*Verity, what the fuck are you doing? You've satisfied your evil curiosity and now know my darkest secret. Why are you still snooping? There's nothing more to see here. Move along now!*

And under that:

*My God, woman, have you nothing better to do?! I have some ideas for a future profession for you: drawer organizer, private detective, handwriting analyst, procrastinator deluxe... SHUT THE FUCKING DRAWER! NOW!*

Finally, under a blue T-shirt with Chewbacca on it, was one last note. Oh, and her missing panties.

*Okay, fine. Yes, I stole your panties. Yes, I was keeping them to rub on myself when you weren't with me. No, I'm not some panty-stealing pervert who does this kind of thing on the regular. You're my first.*
*I just wanted to have a part of you, I guess. Something to remind me how delicate and sweet you are. How I can't get enough of you. How totally sexy and fucking insanely aroused you make me.*
*So, yeah. As tempted as I was to snap a crapload of pictures of you while you slept, I went with the slightly less stalkerish option of stealing your underwear. Sue me.*
*If you're creeped out by me keeping them, then go ahead and take them back. I won't mind.*
*X Hud*

*PS. Please don't take them back. You know I'm capable of breaking into your apartment, right? Leave these where they are, and the entire contents of your underwear drawer will remain safe. For now. Don't make me go all Liam Neeson on your ass. It wouldn't be pretty.*

Verity shook her head, unable to stop smiling.

Okay, so it was official. She loved this man. She loved every part of him—from his hard body and gorgeous face to his passion and intensity. She loved his utterly ridiculous sense of humor and his amazing belief in and devotion to her. He made her feel like she could fly.

And even though this was the first time she'd felt like this about someone, loving him didn't seem weird or scary. In fact, it seemed more natural and right than anything else.

Smiling as she admitted that to herself, Verity was overwhelmed by the need to tell Hudson about her revelation. Right the hell now. She grabbed her phone and quickly dialed his number. It rang three times before he picked up.

"Hey. Can't talk—on a delivery run. I'll call you later, okay?"

She barely had time to open her mouth to reply before the line went dead.

Her shoulders slumped. "Okay. By the way, I'm in love with you."

She sat and stared at the phone for few seconds, disappointed she wouldn't get to shower Hudson with her epic declaration of love until later. Still, she had zero time to wallow. It wasn't like a job was going to throw itself at her. With a final sigh, Verity shoved her phone in her purse, took a last whiff of Hudson's pillow, and left the apartment.

Four hours later and back at her own place, Verity's eyes were drier than the Sahara from leaning over her computer and desperately searching job sites for something she might be qualified for. The more she'd thought about it, the less she wanted to call on her dad for help. She'd introduce him to Hudson when the time was right, but that wouldn't be until she could prove how well her New York life was going. Hence the need to find a new-and-improved job ASAP. However, it seemed that in order to secure a job that paid her anything close to Lay's generous wage, she'd either have to magically come up with a master's degree, or be open to a position in the adult entertainment industry. Well, various positions, really.

She was about to give the entire internet the finger when her phone rang.

A shiver of excitement ran up her spine as she snatched the device and checked caller ID.

*Dammit.* It was only Angie.

"Hey," she said with a level of enthusiasm in the negative digits.

"Wow," Angie said. "Did someone die? Has alcohol been banned? Why do you sound so morose?"

Verity rubbed her eyes. "I'm fine. Sorry. I've been looking for a job, which is a demoralizing process, and I thought you might be Hudson. We haven't spoken today."

Angie chuckled. "Oh, man. You're like a junkie craving her next hit. Girl, you have it so bad for this guy."

There was no use denying it, and yet, Verity tried. "No, not at all. I'm just—you know, he left this morning before I woke up, and I haven't been able to contact him since."

"He's a big boy, honey. He can take care of himself."

"I know that, but—"

"You're twitching like a tweaker because you haven't heard his voice in a few hours?"

Verity sighed. "I'm not twitching. Much."

Angie laughed again. "So forget about him and come out with me and Joseph tonight. We're meeting at our usual spot. We'll hang out, have some laughs, and if Hudson ever pulls his head out of his ass and reappears, he can come join us. What do you say?"

It was tempting. Between her craving for Hudson and a complete lack of viable job prospects that allowed her to pay rent and keep her clothes on, Verity could use a drink. Or five.

"Let me try Hudson one more time, and if he doesn't have plans for us, I'll come."

"Cool. Text me."

"Will do."

After she signed off with Angie, Verity sent Hudson a text.

> Hey. I've missed you today. Want to get together tonight? I have something I need to tell you.

After a couple of minutes, her phone vibrated with his reply.

> Tonight's one of my inconveniently busy nights. But have fun without me!

He ended it with a smiley-face emoji. Verity frowned. Now that she had something to say, it seemed she might never get to say it. She closed her laptop and texted Angie.

> It seems I'm available to grace you with my presence tonight. Let's hope I don't screw anyone in the VIP room this time.

Angie replied:

> Wait, you fucked Hudson in the VIP room? WHY AM I ONLY HEARING ABOUT THIS NOW? See you at 8.

Verity answered:

> The funeral seemed like a bad time to bring it up. Can't wait to see you.

Verity smiled and opened Twitter:

**Verity Michaels** @VerityPics03
Happiness is being happy with who you are. Then you find the other half of your heart as a reward #RewardIsAlsoSex

# Chapter 23

## New Kickass Verity
## Leisa Rayven

That evening, as Angie and Verity made their way through the crowd to the bar, a tall guy with a beard stepped in front of them.

"Hey, sweetheart," he said, leering at Verity. "What happened to your outfit from the other night? I liked it better than this look."

Verity smiled at him. "Yeah? Well, I liked your personality better before you opened your mouth. And newsflash: I don't choose clothes to please you. So back off."

Verity pushed past him, and Angie followed, smirking openly.

"I'm not sure if it's your liberated job status, all the sex, or your frustration over missing Hudson, but I'm enjoying this new Verity. She's kickass."

"Yeah?" Verity said. "Maybe I'm finally getting myself some New York attitude. Hudson is rubbing off on me." She sighed. "Or I could be delirious with unemployment paranoia.

Man or no man, I have no idea what I'm going to do."

"Well, I have something that will help with that."

Angie leaned over and got the bartender's attention. "Six shots of tequila, Jonah. Wait..." She turned to assess Verity, then turned back. "Better make that eight."

Jonah nodded knowingly, then set a row of shot glasses out in front of them, along with some salt and lime wedges, and filled them up. "Have a good time, ladies."

Angie turned to Verity. "If you're still tense after all of these, there's no hope. Off you go. Lick, sip, and suck your way to happiness."

*Sometimes it's almost that simple.* Verity giggled to herself before downing the first shot. She hissed as the tequila burn hit her. "So, where's Joseph tonight? I thought he was coming."

"He is," Angie said. "He just had to finish up some work."

After another shot, Verity studied her friend. "So what's going on with you two, anyway? You've been spending a hell of a lot of time together."

Angie shrugged. "I like him."

"Are you sleeping with him now? I seem to recall a hazy discussion of that the other night."

Angie's expression dropped. "You know, I still have no idea how to answer that question."

"Uh, you don't know if you're sleeping together? Because... ew."

"No!" Angie leaned in and lowered her voice. "Okay, so I haven't told you about this because I don't know what to make of it, but..." She looked over her shoulder before turning back toward Verity. "Joe and I went to high school together, and I had the biggest crush on him, but I had a boyfriend at the time, so nothing happened. Then he went off to college, and we lost touch, but since he's moved back here for his swanky new job—he's some kind of design and engineering consultant—we've been hanging out again."

"Yeah," said Verity. "I've noticed. So where's the weird part?"

"Well, we've been making out for weeks now, and he always goes down on me. I mean, he's down there *a lot*. But whenever I try to return the favor, he bails. That's weird, right? A guy who doesn't like his dick being sucked is about as rare as a unicorn that plays hockey. Am I right?"

Verity nodded. "In my limited experience? Absolutely."

"So what the hell? I mean, like Baby in *Dirty Dancing*, my vag has had the time of her life, but Joe doesn't want to do anything else? Honestly, if he didn't have the world's most talented tongue, I'd kick him to the curb."

Angie handed Verity another shot, and they knocked them back. Angie was still sucking on her lime when her phone beeped with a message.

"Speak of the devil," she muttered. "He's just arrived."

Angie did their last two shots by herself, which was fine, as Verity had already arrived at the line between pleasantly buzzed and sloppy drunk and come to a hard stop. Angie, however, ordered another row and had conquered one more shot before Joseph arrived and leaned on the bar beside her.

"Ladies. What did I miss?"

"Nothing," Angie said, looking at him with bleary eyes. "But these are our shots. You'll have to get your own."

Joseph smiled at her. "Sweetheart, you've already hit your limit. I'm going to have to confiscate these for your own safety."

He downed two shots in quick succession and shook his head. "That's better."

"Bad day?" Verity asked.

Joseph pulled out his phone and quickly scanned an email. "You could say that. Just some unexpected complications—someone trying to hack my internet. Nothing life threatening."

Angie took his phone from him and slid it into her impressive cleavage. "Well, you're here now, so forget work and dance with me."

Joseph downed another shot and slid his arm around her waist. "Yes, ma'am." He winked at Verity as they pushed through the crowd toward the dance floor.

Verity watched them for a while, partly because drunk-Angie dancing was funny as hell, but also because Joseph had some surprisingly cool moves. When Verity was hit with a sudden pang of missing Hudson, she took out her phone to check Twitter. Her heart skipped a beat when she saw she had new mentions.

**Hudson Fenn** @tatwhiteknight
When did tweets about a chick finding her heart become so hot? Torn between staying away to inspire more, or giving her what she wants. @VerityPics03

"Give her what she wants," Verity whispered to the phone. "For the love of God, put her out of her misery."

**Hudson Fenn** @tatwhiteknight
FOUND: One horny-as-hell boyfriend. Looking for GF. All information can be directed to my pants. #BonerInWaiting

*Oh, as soon as you show your face, I'm all over your pants, mister,* Verity thought. *Have no doubt.*

**Hudson Fenn** @tatwhiteknight
"I Want To Know What Love Is," is on the radio. Appropriate. #IWantYouToShowMe #PSILoveYou

Verity stopped breathing. *What was... I mean he didn't just...? Seriously?*

With shaking fingers, she replied:

**Verity Michaels** @VerityPics03
You did NOT just tell me you loved me over Twitter?

**Hudson Fenn** @tatwhiteknight
Didn't I? I thought I did. My mistake #ILoveYouVerity

## #OopsIdidItAgain #ThoughtYouShouldKnow

**Verity Michaels** @VerityPics03
HUDSON FENN!

Verity nearly jumped out of her skin when warm lips grazed her ear and a deep voice whispered, "Yes?"

She turned to find him, smirking and gorgeous. She threw herself at him and claimed his mouth like he'd claimed her heart.

He grunted at her unexpected attack, but within seconds he was pressing her up against the bar as he kissed her back.

"How did it go?" Verity asked between kisses.

"Quiet, woman," Hudson ordered. "You can't talk and have my tongue in your mouth at the same time, and right now, I need that second thing to happen."

He kissed her again, deeply, and every ounce of oxygen in Verity's lungs disappeared as he stroked his tongue against hers, the smooth ball making her shiver. His strong arms encircled her, crushing her against him.

*Oh, Lord.* The feel of him. The smell. The storm of electricity that fired between their bodies. All of it, combined with the alcohol in her system, made her giddy and breathless.

She pulled back and closed her eyes as she regained her breath.

"You okay, Honeybee?" he asked. "I didn't hurt you, did I?"

"No." Verity opened her eyes and smiled. "I'm amazing. More than amazing. And for the record, I'm in love with you, too."

A breathtaking smile lit up Hudson's face. "Yeah?"

"Yeah. I mean, I don't have your romantic flair for broadcasting it on social media or anything, but—"

That's as far as she got before Hudson was kissing her again. One of his hands slid down to her ass, and Verity moaned as he pressed his very obvious erection into her leg.

"Let's get out of here," he said, his voice low and breathy. "Because I need to be inside you right the hell now, and there's no way I'm risking my genital health in the VIP room again. That's just asking for gonorrhea."

Verity rested her hands on the hard muscles of his chest. "Seconded. But let me find Angie. I should tell her."

Just then, Angie appeared beside them.

"Well, what do you know?" she said, looking Hudson up and down. "If it isn't *Hud*ini." She leaned into him. "See what I did there? Hudini instead of Houdini? 'Cause you keep disappearing."

Hudson chuckled. "Yeah, I got that. Very clever."

"So whass the story, morning glory? Where have you been, big guy?"

Angie stumbled against him, and Hudson steadied her. "Clearly not at the bottom of a tequila bottle like you, Ang. How about you sit down before you fall down?"

Angie scowled. "I'm not drunk, I'll have you know. I'm serfectly pober." She frowned. "Wait, that didn't come out right."

Verity touched her friend's shoulder. "We're going to bail, honey. You probably should, too."

Angie swayed a little. "Yeah, my work here is done. Joe just needed to see the bar manager about some function he wants to organize next week, so I told him I'd meet him outside."

Verity nodded. "Cool. I'll meet you guys out the front after I run to the ladies' room."

Hudson gave Verity a soft kiss. "Pee fast. You have no idea what kind of pain I'm in right now."

Verity grazed her hand over the bulge in his jeans. "Oh, believe me, I do."

Hudson hissed as she made her way to the back of the club.

After the world's most satisfying pee, Verity washed up and was about to head back through the crowd when she heard groaning.

She cocked her head and listened more closely. It was masked by the rest of the noise from the bar, but it was definitely there. She moved down the hallway toward the sound, and as she reached a supply closet, it got louder.

*Oh my God! Are there people actually screwing in there? Anything can happen in Manhattan, apparently.*

The door to the closet was open slightly, and when she peeked through, her heart jumped to her throat. Leaning against a set of shelves that held toilet paper and cleaning supplies was Joseph. His pants and underwear were around his ankles, and in front of him—on her knees—was one of the bartenders, deep throating him like a pro.

*Dear God. That girl really will do anything for a good tip.* Verity pulled back, her mind racing. *So Joseph won't go all the way with Angie because... he's a cheater? But then why all the lady head? It doesn't make sense.*

Her stomach churned as she headed out of the club. She had to tell Angie, didn't she? She couldn't let her friend carry on

*Felony* Ever After

with a dude who was getting sexed up by other women in broom closets. That was all kinds of unacceptable.

Verity was still pondering her options when she reached the parking lot. She saw Hudson leaning against his car and headed over.

When she got there, she looked around. "Where's Angie?"

Hudson opened the back door to reveal Angie passed out on the cream leather. "Princess Tequila has fallen into an inebriated slumber. Guess I'm the designated driver, huh?"

He was about to say something else when his phone rang. He pulled it from his pocket and checked caller ID before holding up one finger to Verity. "One second. I have to take this. I'll be right back." He turned his back on her. "Hey, Daniel. What's up?"

As he walked out of earshot, Verity sighed and checked her phone. Seemed the thing to do.

Hudson had sent her another tweet:

**Hudson Fenn** @tatwhiteknight
Just so you know, 140 characters isn't nearly enough space to tell you how amazing I think you are.

**Hudson Fenn** @tatwhiteknight
So later, I'll write an essay. On your body. With my tongue.

Verity was still beaming like an idiot when she heard footsteps behind her.

She turned to see Joseph, slightly red-faced, but smiling.

No, not smiling. Grinning—like a man who'd just blown his load into the mouth of a particularly attractive member of the hospitality industry.

"Everyone ready to go?" he asked.

Verity grimaced. She had to tell him she knew. "Joseph, listen, I—"

Out of nowhere, Hudson stormed into view, and before Verity even had time to register the murderous expression on his face, he'd grabbed Joseph by the front of his shirt and thrown him into the side of the car.

"You piece of shit!"

Hudson slammed his fist into Joseph's jaw, and when Joseph collapsed onto the pavement, Hudson stood over him, fists clenched. "Hand over your phone, you fuck!"

Joseph looked up at him in shock. "The hell are you doing, Fenn? What's wrong with you?"

Hudson disappeared to the back of the car and opened the trunk. A few seconds later, he reappeared, holding a tire iron. He glared at Joseph with barely contained fury.

"Give me your phone, right the fuck now, or I start breaking bones. Your choice."

"Hudson—" Verity placed a hand on his shoulder. He shrugged her off.

"Stay back, Verity. This is between me and this man-shaped piece of shit."

Joseph stared up at Hudson. He looked about ready to pee

himself.

"Phone!" Hudson ordered again, his hand outstretched.

Joseph fumbled in his pocket and handed it over.

Hudson stood stone-faced as he fiddled with it. Whatever he saw made his already furious expression darken into a full head of storm clouds.

"What's going on?" Angie mumbled as she emerged from car.

Hudson turned to her, so angry he was trembling.

"What's going on, Angie, is that your boyfriend here is a grade A, platinum-plated asshole, who was about to sell your likeness and your vagina to the highest bidder."

He held out Joseph's phone, and on the screen was a picture of a sex doll—a sex doll that looked exactly like Angie.

Angie's face fell. "What the hell am I looking at right now?"

She scrolled through the pictures, and with each one, she looked more and more like she was going to throw up.

"Joseph?" She was on the verge of tears.

Hudson grabbed Joseph's shirt and forced him up against the side of the car. "After everything that went on with Verity, and Lay, and his stupid allegations, I knew someone was stealing from my uncle's company. I did some digging, and it turns out Joseph here has been moonlighting."

Verity and Angie looked at Hudson in confusion. Hudson continued to stare daggers at Joseph. "He took a consulting job with my uncle's company, helping them develop new technology for the dolls. But then he went rogue." Hudson turned to Verity. "Remember the first time I met him, he said I looked familiar?" She nodded. "That's because we were at MIT together. *He's* the MIT graduate Lay was talking about."

"Oh my God."

Hudson turned back to Joseph, who wasn't denying anything. "Anyway, he seems to have liberated some proprietary information and confidential details provided by HoneyBee clients. He's been making knock-off dolls using real women as the models—women who never agreed to be mass produced. He stole most of the likenesses, but looks like lately he'd been feeling super creative. You were the next one to be produced, Angie. Your whole profile is in a draft folder on Joseph's home computer. My friend Daniel is a hacker, and he's been working all day to find the source of the transactions for knock-off dolls. He just cracked it, and it all leads back to Joey-boy here."

Verity glared at Joseph. "So that's why you kept going down on her? For, what? Research? You piece of—"

Angie walked over to Joseph, seeming sobered by the information, and gave him a wounded look. "Joe? Is this true?"

Joseph glanced at Hudson before coming back to Angie. He seemed to decide lying wasn't an option at this point. Hudson looked like he would break both his legs if he even breathed wrong right now.

"It's true. HoneyBee's dolls are beautiful, and it's a waste that they're all just one of a kind. They're leaving piles of money on the table by not making their best ladies more widely available. So I started making a few more on my own." He paused to sneer at Hudson. "They're far from mass produced."

"I doubt that will matter a whole lot to the women whose privacy has been violated, jackhole," Verity snapped. "Angie doesn't want random copies of herself in anyone's bedroom at all!"

Joseph turned to Angie, a pleading look in his eyes. "Men

who are into dolls are incredibly fussy, so I knew only the most beautiful women would do. Angie, ever since high school, you've been the most beautiful woman I know. It had to be you. Your doll would have made me rich. Well, richer."

Angie's voice wavered as she held back tears. "That's supposed to make me feel better about being turned into a sex toy? That you think I'm beautiful?"

Quick as lightning, she grabbed him by the shoulders and slammed her knee into his groin. "Fuck you, Joe." He grunted and collapsed to his knees as Angie stood over him. "I hope Hudson's uncle sues you down to your last dollar, you pathetic piece of crap."

Joseph fell to his side and groaned.

"Oh, have no fear, he's ruined," Hudson said. "He's in breach of so many patents and copyrights, it's not even funny. My uncle's lawyers are going to have a field day."

Hudson put his arm around Angie and helped her back into the car. As he walked around to open the door for Verity, he called over to Joseph:

"Just FYI, douchebag, I'm keeping your phone. See you in court."

With that, he climbed into the car, and they screamed away, leaving Joseph clutching his ruined balls.

Verity took one last look at Angie asleep in her bed before pulling her bedroom door closed. She turned to where Hudson leaned against her kitchen counter, sipping coffee.

"She okay?" he asked.

Verity nodded. "In a way, she's relieved. She knew something wasn't right about him, and now she knows the truth. What I didn't tell her is that I saw Joseph having his dick sucked earlier by the bartender at the Library Bar."

Hudson's eyebrows rose. "Seriously? The blonde with the triple-D implants?"

Verity grimaced. "Yup."

Hudson put his coffee down on the counter. "Oh, shit. Well, maybe it's best she doesn't find out about that."

"Agreed."

Hudson wrapped Verity in his arms. She sighed and leaned into his chest. "This has been quite a week," he said. "But the mystery of the knock-off sex dolls has been solved. We should be proud. We laid rubber Verity to rest, saved women from being exploited, recovered my uncle's reputation, and created enough work to keep his lawyers busy for years."

"Yes, if those were paid positions, I'd consider myself gainfully employed," Verity said with a laugh. "Although you did most of the work."

"Everyone needs a sidekick," Hudson said, his eyes twinkling. "So, what did you do today apart from miss me?"

Verity closed her eyes. "Oh, you know. Had deep philosophical discussions with your cats, scavenged through your drawers and fell in love with you via your hidden Star Wars obsession, looked all over the internet for jobs that don't exist. The usual."

Hudson chuckled and kissed the top of her head. "Really? It was the 1970s nerd paraphernalia that finally tipped the balance in my favor? Sounds like a full day. One question: Did you leave the panties where they were? Or do I have to go on an underwear rampage before I leave this apartment?"

Verity looked up at him. "No, my panties now have an exciting new home with your Star Wars buddies; all my undies should be so lucky."

Hudson smiled. "Excellent." He kissed her gently, then pulled back and stared down at her. "So, do you need to stay here with your friend? Or can I convince you to come back to my place for a night of fun and orgasms?"

Verity extricated herself from Hudson's arms. "I should really stay. I don't want Angie to think I've abandoned her in her hour of need. But you know, my couch is also a sofabed. You could stay here."

Hudson frowned. "Hmmm. Sleeping on a lumpy sofabed with you, or snuggling into my king-sized bed alone. Tough choice. I'd like to phone a friend."

She rolled her eyes, and Hudson smiled as he picked up a folder from her coffee table. He pulled out the collection of photos and flicked through them. "What's this?"

"Oh, the photography part of my resume, I guess. I dragged everything out for the job search today." Verity nodded. "Not sure there's anything in there that says *pay me a living wage*, though, right?" Hudson didn't answer. He just stared at her pictures.

"I'm not kidding when I say there are no jobs I'm even remotely qualified for in the greater New York area." Still nothing. "So I'm looking at starting an exciting new career in the adult film industry." She paused. "I mean, I know I'll have to figure out which is the best side of my vagina and all, so they can light it appropriately, but being able to write off Brazilians as a tax deduction? Worth it."

"Uh-huh." Hudson now studied one picture in particular.

"Yep," Verity said. "Can't wait to get me some professional cock. All day, every day. Nomnomnom."

At that, Hudson looked up. "What the fuck did you just say?"

Verity smiled. "Nothing. Just lamenting my lack of job prospects."

"What do you mean?" he asked, holding up the pictures. "Here's your job. *This.* Verity Michaels: professional photographer."

Verity raised an eyebrow. "Really? I couldn't make that work in Florida, but you think New York is dying for me?"

He gave her an incredulous look. "I know they're dying for you, Country Girl. And I'd be happy to help them realize it. These are amazing. You know, my clients are sometimes looking for tattoo inspiration," he said, dropping his voice to top-secret level. "Not to mention some arty shots of their latest work. I know that's among your skills…"

He trailed off meaningfully, and Verity's mouth hung open. She could feel a happy dance starting in her toes.

"Get your portfolio together—in something other than a folder on your coffee table—and there'll be no stopping you," Hudson added. "You're really fucking talented, and I'm not just saying that because I don't want you to become the biggest female star the adult film industry has ever known."

"I thought you weren't listening."

"Please. You were talking about fucking other men. I was

Felony Ever After

about three seconds away from tattooing my name on your ass so everyone knows you're mine."

He pulled her into his side and gestured to the pictures. "Speaking of tattoos, can I steal some of these? I know people with money to spend who would go batshit crazy if I converted these images into tats."

Verity rested her head on his chest and breathed in his incredible scent. "Of course. You can be my first client. Take whatever you want."

Without warning, Hudson scooped her up into his arms. She squealed and gripped his shoulders. "Hudson! What the—?"

He pressed his lips softly against hers. "You told me to take whatever I wanted. Well, newsflash: what I want is you." He turned to look at the couch. "Now, on a scale of one to screaming-my-name, exactly how much noise can we make out here without waking Angie?"

Verity laughed as Hudson threw her on the couch and proceeded to kiss the hell out of her as he removed her clothes. Needless to say, the next day, Verity had one of the happiest vaginas on the planet.

**Hudson Fenn** @tatwhiteknight
Believing in her is the easiest thing in the world. #GreatRackToo

# 1 Story 13 Authors

**Verity Michaels** @VerityPictures03
My special tatted white knight. You make dreaming that much easier. #GiantDickToo

**Verity Michaels** @VerityPictures03
We are going to make our followers gag with the sweet talk. #ThatGivesMeAnIdea

**Hudson Fenn** @tatwhiteknight
Well now you gave me and my giant dick that idea. Come closer. #ComeAgain

# Epilogue

### Out of Parole
### Belle Aurora

One month later, a knock on Verity's apartment door sounded just after eight p.m. She approached with caution and checked the peephole.

The wide, dimpled grin on the other side of it had her returning it full force.

She threw the door open, smiling apologetically. "I'm sorry. We don't want any," then moved to close it in his face.

"Hey," Hudson used his shoulder to push his way in. "Is that what I get for bringing you pizza?"

The smell hit her like a wave. Cheese, basil, rich tomato sauce, and *Hudson* had her salivating. *Did I eat today?*

"Mmmm," Verity hummed. "I'm shocked to see you at the door. Can't hack getting a pizza through the window?"

Hudson placed the box on the kitchen counter and stalked over to her. "Mmmm," he purred in response. "Shush your pretty mouth."

Verity had a feeling the pizza wasn't as heavy on his mind as it was hers. She confirmed this when he gripped her hips lightly, moving her back until she was trapped against the refrigerator. His warm lips brushed hers, and she felt her body respond.

In an instant, Verity was ready. As in, Betty-Crocker-Super-Moist-cake *ready*.

Her eyes closed, and she deepened the kiss, standing on her tiptoes and twining her arms around his neck just to feel him. When they separated, his eyes were hooded with lust, just as her own likely were.

"Wow," Hudson drawled.

Her arms still around his neck, she told him her news. "I got two more clients today."

It seemed to take him a second to process what she'd said. When it sunk in, his brows rose. "You did? Make that three, because I've got someone interested in one of your images."

Hudson's smile was beautiful. Her victories were his victories. She loved that about them. Without warning, he dipped low and lifted her. Verity had no choice but to hold on. She squeaked then snorted. "What are you doing?"

He rushed them to the bedroom. "Celebrating."

They celebrated long and hard into the night, though she did manage to talk him into a pizza break. Verity couldn't remember sex ever feeling this way before, the way it did with Hudson. Perhaps that was because with Hudson, it was more.

As the celebration wound down, Verity and Hudson lay in bed, watching each other in the moonlight. Hudson took Verity's hand, pulled it close and kissed her knuckles, whisper soft. "What are you thinking, Honeybee?"

"I'm going to have to move. I'm not going to be able to afford this place on a freelance photographer's salary—at least not right away," Verity pondered out loud. "I shouldn't blow through all of my severance cash." Then she grinned. "So you want to help me search for a new place? Or I might have to get a roommate."

Hudson smiled, slow and sly. "I could help you search," he began. "Or you could just come live with me."

Verity's heart skipped a beat. "Oh yeah?" she breathed.

He kissed her knuckles again, his mouth lingering. She felt his cool grin on her skin. "Yeah. But just as roomies, like you said. You know, two people who live together and have great sex. That sort of thing."

Verity's brows rose and she laughed. "Two people who live together and have sex—"

"*Great* sex," he corrected.

"Right. And go on dates. That sort of thing."

Hudson nodded, a look of mock relief coming over him. "Exactly. You get it." He ran his thumb over her lips. "Just two people who live together and have sex and go on dates." His voice turned quiet. "And who sleep in the same room." He leaned over to kiss her smiling mouth. "And have fun together." His lips moved from her mouth to her cheek to her jaw. "And make a life together."

Verity's smile stretched so far she thought her face would split.

Hudson looked into Verity's eyes and shot her those dimples. "You moving in with me, Honeybee?"

How could she resist?

"Yeah, Tattoo," she responded. "I think I will."

**Verity Michaels** @VerityPics03
#MaybeFelonsArentSoBad #DreamsCanComeTrue
#MovingInwithMyMan

**Hudson Fenn** @tatwhiteknight
#VerityAndHudsonForever #HoneybeeAndTattoo
#NOHO

**Verity Michaels** @VerityPics03
#HappilyEverAfterWithAFelon
#TheEnd

Follow **Verity** on Twitter:
https://twitter.com/VerityPics03

Follow **Hudson** on Twitter:
https://twitter.com/tatwhiteknight

Visit **SalesExportt.com** for more book fun and see the trailer!

# About the Author
# Helena Hunting

NYT and USA Today bestselling author of The Pucked Series, Helena Hunting lives on the outskirts of Toronto with her incredibly tolerant family and two moderately intolerant cats. She's writes contemporary romance ranging from new adult angst to romantic sports comedy.

SAVE THE DATE: MARCH 29th Alex and Violet tie the knot… but not on a cape, Violet's learned her lesson—Velcro only this time.

### Forever Pucked

Being engaged to Alex Waters, team captain and the highest paid NHL player in the league, is awesome. How could it not be?

In addition to being an amazing hockey player, he's an incurable romantic with an XL heart, and an XXL hockey stick in his pants. And he knows how to use it. Incredibly, orgasmically well. Alex is the whole package and more. Literally. Like his package is insane. Total world record holder material.

So it makes complete sense that Violet Hall can't wait to nail him down to the matrimonial mattress and become Mrs. Violet Waters.

It's so romantic.

Violet is totally stoked to set a date. Eventually. At some point. Likely before the next millennium. Or when Violet stops getting hives every time someone brings up the wedding, and their mothers stop colluding on stadium sized venues. Whichever comes first.

## FOREVER PUCKED EXCERPT

Charlene, my best friend and colleague at Stroker and Cobb Financial Management, peeks her head into my cubicle. She looks disembodied with the way the rest of her is out of sight. She's also smiling like she belongs in some kind of asylum.

"What's up?" I ask.

"You have a delivery."

"What kind of delivery?"

Alex likes to send me gifts at work. Once he had some guy dressed as a beaver sing a love song to me. It was mortifying. Jimmy, one of the other junior accountants, recorded it and posted it on YouTube. Obviously I made him take it down, but it had already gone viral.

"An Alex delivery."

I brace myself for humiliation as she grunts, moving my gift into view.

I don't say anything for a few long seconds. Alex is over the top with everything. But then, when you're the highest-paid NHL player in the league, you can afford to be extravagant and highly ridiculous.

"Not what you expected?" Charlene asks, biting her lip to keep from busting out laughing.

"What am I supposed to do with this?" I gesture to the four-foot stuffed beaver wearing a hockey jersey. It's almost as wide as it is tall.

## Other Books By Helena Hunting

**PUCKED SERIES**
Pucked (Pucked #1)
Pucked Up (Pucked #2)
Pucked Over (Pucked #3)
Forever Pucked (Pucked #4 Spring 2016)

**THE CLIPPED WINGS SERIES**
Cupcakes and Ink
Clipped Wings
Between the Cracks
Inked Armor
Cracks in the Armor

**STANDALONE NOVELS**
The Librarian Principle

**Connect with Helena**

**Website:**
www.helenahunting.com

# About the Author
# Penelope Ward

Penelope Ward is a New York Times, USA Today and #1 Wall Street Journal bestselling author. She grew up in Boston with five older brothers and spent most of her twenties as a television news anchor before switching to a more family-friendly career.

Penelope lives for reading books in the new adult/contemporary romance genre, coffee and hanging out with her friends and family on weekends. She is the proud mother of a beautiful 11-year-old girl with autism (the inspiration for the character Callie in Gemini) and a 9-year-old boy, both of whom are the lights of her life.

Penelope, her husband and kids reside in Rhode Island.

She is the author of RoomHate, which hit #2 on the New York Times Bestseller list and #1 on the Wall Street Journal Bestseller list. Her novel, Stepbrother Dearest, also spent four consecutive weeks on the New York Times Bestseller list. Other works include the New York Times bestseller Cocky Bastard (co-written with Vi Keeland), Sins of Sevin, My Skylar, Jake Undone, Jake Understood and Gemini.

## Connect with Penelope

### Website:
### www.penelopewardauthor.com

# About the Author
# Tijan

I didn't start writing till later in life. I hope I'm doing it right, and if not, I'll continue to keep trying! Nothing special about me. I've got an English Cocker that I absolutely adore, a man I couldn't be without, and this insatiable need to keep writing the words, all the words!

**Keep track of me through Facebook at Tijan's Books!**

**Connect with Tijan**

**Website:**
**www.tijansbooks.com**

WALLSTREET JOURNAL, NEW YORK TIMES, AND USA TODAY BESTSELLING AUTHOR

# About the Author
# Katherine Stevens

When Katherine Stevens isn't writing, she can usually be found opening juice boxes and looking for lost shoes. Her kids keep her quite busy and always zig-zagging across the line of sanity. She is a lifelong Texan with a terrible sense of direction and even worse memory. She thinks life is entirely too hard if you don't laugh your way through it. As a child, she dreamed of being the most sarcastic astronaut in history, but her poor math skills and aversion to dehydrated food kept her out of the space program. Now she writes to pass the time until NASA lowers their standards. Your move, NASA.

Her next novel GOING DOWN releases spring 2016!

The plan for Cici Carrington was to steadily climb UP the corporate ladder, and hopefully do so without her skirt tucked into the back of her underpants.

Unfortunately, there was no contingency plan for the aftermath of spending a night trapped in an elevator with a suit-wearing Elevator Sex God named Cole Danvers. A one… or two-time dalliance wouldn't normally throw off the course of someone's life… unless you find out you have to work together the next day.

To further complicate matters, Cici's best friend is also her Human Resources Director. She has to hide her secret from every person she knows. Her only confidant is her one-eyed cat, and his loyalty is tenuous at best. Toss in an accidental mugging, a bungled disguise, secret meetings, and unintentional arson, and Cici's beautiful, careful plan has fallen by the wayside.

Perhaps there aren't any hard and fast rules in life. Sometimes you can have your cake and eat it too. Sometimes following the rules doesn't get you ahead.

And perhaps sometimes you can get off between floors...

**Connect with Katherine**

**Website:**
**www.authorkatherinestevens.com**

# About the Author
# KA Robinson

KA. Robinson is the New York Times and USA Today best-selling author of several New Adult and Contemporary Romance novels. She is both self-published and traditionally published through Atria Books (Torn and Twisted). She is represented by Jane Dystel of Dystel and Goderich Literary Agency.

She lives in West Virginia with her toddler son. Her addictions include books, Supernatural, Sons of Anarchy, coffee, and Rock Music.

**Connect with KA**

**Website:**
**www.authorkarobinson.com**

# About the Author
# Liesa Rayven

Writing has always been a passion for Leisa, and even though she originally intended to be an actress, it wasn't long into her time at drama school that she began writing plays. Those plays were bad. Very bad. Well, her friends thought they were good, but that's because they were always cast in them and any opportunity to be on stage was met with an obnoxious amount of enthusiasm.

Since then, she's honed her craft, and several of her plays have been produced and toured throughout Australia.

These days, playwriting has given way to fiction writing, and Leisa's debut novel, BAD ROMEO, was published through Macmillan New York in December 2014. The sequel, BROKEN JULIET was released in April 2015, and the final book in Leisa's Starcrossed series, WICKED HEART, will hit bookstores and kindles on May 3rd, 2016.

The Starcrossed series has gained hordes of passionate fans all over the world, and the books have now been translated into eight foreign languages. *Bad Romeo* and *Broken Juliet* have also featured on international best seller lists in Brazil and Germany.

Leisa Rayven lives in Australia with her husband, two little boys, three cats, and a kangaroo named Howard.

(Howard may or may not be her imaginary marsupial friend. Everyone should have one.)

**Connect with Leisa**
**Website:**
**www.leisarayven.com**

# About the Author
# Liv Morris
### Coming April 25th, 2016:
### MARRY SCREW KILL

Raised in the Ozark Mountains of Missouri, Liv Morris now resides on St. Croix, USVI with her first and hopefully last husband. After relocating twelve times during his corporate career, she qualifies as a professional mover. Learning to bloom where she's planted, Liv brings her moving and life experience to her writing.

**Connect with Liv**

**Website:**
www.livmorris.com

# About the Author
## SM Lumetta

S.M. Lumetta is a novelist and graphic designer living in New York City. She owns a ridiculous number of t-shirts, and expects Oxford University to be calling any day to honor her with a doctorate in sarcasm.

**Connect with SM**

**Website:**
**www.smlumetta.com**

Her first novel, YOU ARE HERE, is a contemporary romantic suspense, expected to release fall 2016. A short excerpt follows:

"Why does the past feel so heavy, so tiring?" I let the question spill out into the air between us. "There was some good stuff. It wasn't all trauma and violence."

I listened to him inhale; his lungs seemed to fill with troubled thoughts. "The good stuff weighs more," he said with a heavy sigh and sad eyes. "That's why it's easier to run away if you leave it behind. But we still waste ourselves trying to change the impossible, only to end up broken and worthless."

His words were painful as they filtered through my skin and into my bones. "You are not—"

"Sorry," he said too quickly for me to finish my chastisement. "We're not talking about me. You probably want to rest and sort through all this stuff. I'm gonna go."

He jumped up from his seat and smoothed the wrinkles on his shirt as he walked toward the front hallway. Confused, it took me a moment before I jumped up and chased after him.

"Stay," I nearly shouted. I grabbed the back of his shirt and tugged. "Please?"

He stopped, but took too long to turn around. I skittered around him and pressed my back to the door, as if I could block him if he really wanted to go.

"I don't really want to be alone right now," I said. I sounded as desperate as he looked, though perhaps for different reasons. I couldn't figure out the reason for the dark cloud surrounding, but its presence pricked at my skin. His chest rose and fell quickly, his eyes tracking all over my body. When we finally locked eyes, the look in his made me feel like prey.

His body slammed into me and I gasped. When he took my lips, the kiss was overpowering and possessive but needy at the same time. I was taken aback, but even more so, it turned me on. Sex was a perfect distraction from the anxiety I was feeling. And given the handful of experience I've had with him, I knew it would be consuming.

# About the Author
## Vi Keeland

Vi Keeland is a native New Yorker with three children that occupy most of her free time, which she complains about often, but wouldn't change for the world. She is an attorney and a *New York Times*, *Wall Street Journal*, & *USA Today* Bestselling author. Over the last three years, ten of her titles have appeared on the *USA Today* Bestseller lists and three on the *New York Times* Bestseller lists.

**Connect with Vi**

**Website:**
www.vikeeland.com

# About the Author
# JM Darhower

J.M. Darhower is the USA Today Bestselling Author of paranormal/erotic/romantic suspense novels about the baddest bad boys and the ladies who love with them. She lives in a tiny town in North Carolina, where she churns out more words than will ever see the light of day. She has a deep passion for politics and speaking out against human trafficking, and when she isn't writing she's usually ranting about those things.

### Connect with JM

### Website:
### www.JMDarhower.com

### Other Works

**Sempre**
**Sempre: Redemption**
**MADE: A Sempre Novel**
**Friends & Forever: Sempre Novellas**

**Monster in His Eyes**
**Torture to Her Soul**
**Target on Our Backs**

**Extinguish**
**Reignite**

**By Any Other Name**
**The Mad Tatter**
**Snowflakes & Fire Escapes**

# About the Author
# Nina Bocci

Nina Bocci is a novelist, publicist, eternal optimist, unabashed lipgloss enthusiast, constant apologist, and a hopeless romanticist. She has too many college degrees that she's not using and a Lego addiction that she blames on her son.

**Her next novel is ROMAN CRAZY with AliceClayton (Gallery Books 9/13/16)**

A delicious, sexy, laugh-out-loud modern romance about a newly single woman and her journey to find love again, from *New York Times* bestselling author Alice Clayton and debut author Nina Bocci.

Avery Bardot steps off the plane in Rome, looking for a fresh start. She's left behind a soon-to-be ex-husband in Boston and plans to spend the summer with her best friend Daisy, licking her wounds—and perhaps a gelato or two. But when her American-expat friend throws her a welcome party on her first night, Avery's thrown for a loop when she sees a man she never thought she'd see again: Italian architect Marcello Bianchi.

Marcello was *the* man—the one who got away. And now her past is colliding with her present, a present where she should be mourning the loss of her marriage and—hey, that fettuccine is delicious! And so is Marcello…

Slipping easily into the good life of summertime in Rome,

Avery spends her days exploring a city that makes art historians swoon, and her nights swooning over her unexpected *what was old is new again* romance. It's heady, it's fevered, it's wanton, and it's crazy. But could this really be her new life? Or is it just a temporary reprieve before returning to the land of twin-set cardigans and crustless sandwiches?

A celebration of great friendship, passionate romance, and wonderful food, *Roman Crazy* is a lighthearted story of second chances and living life to the fullest.

## Unedited, subject to change ROMAN CRAZY by Alice Clayton & Nina Bocci (Gallery 9/13/16)

### Roman Crazy

He let me soak up Rome in my own way. To capture it like an artist would. I asked questions when they arose but for the most part, he led and I followed enjoying the company and the atmosphere. When I mentioned feeling a bit hungry, he bought me a bag full of little fried fish, tossed with lemon and salt, delicious.

We'd kept to a safe distance, only an occasional shoulder brush, maybe his hand in the small of back to steer me around something but still, a respectable arms length.

But as night began to creep in, and the light was changing to a rich warm last bit of sun more like a candelight glow, it became harder and harder to ignore the powerful draw that was still there, still between us. That string was still there tethering me, us, to the memories of Barcelona. He'd kept things on a very friendly level all day, but here, in the narrow alley between bustling piazzas, his struggle was magnified. He seemed too big for the space with his broad chest heaving and devilish Roman smirk melting away my resistance to the idea of a fling with him again. Wait, was I resisting?

I felt an invisible hand at my back nudging me toward him. It was like the walls behind us were pushing us together. Any closer and these flimsy walls I mentally built would be toast.

"Marcello?" I asked, reaching out to touch his forearm. I loved the feeling of the muscles bunching and pulling as his hand flexed into a fist.

He was struggling. His eyebrows bunched, lips pursed and his eyes swung to my hand on his arm. I shouldn't have enjoyed it but I did.

Did he want to touch me as much as I wanted to let him?

**Connect with Nina**
**Website:**
**ninabocci.com**

# About the Author
# Belle Aurora

USA Today Bestselling author Belle Aurora was born in the land down under.

At an early age she fell in love with reading. Boredom one summer had her scouring the bookshelves at home. She stumbled across Sandra Brown's Breath of Scandal and fell in love with romance.

Having been brought up in a loud and boisterous family of Croatian descent, she developed a natural love for dramatics and humor. Only some years ago had she discovered a new love.

Humorous romance novels.

Kristen Ashley and R.L. Mathewson had opened a brand new world where she could lose herself yet feel safe and at home in their stories. Belle has been known to become a screeching banshee while anxiously awaiting their newest titles.

Belle never thought she would write. It had never interested her until recently. Friend-Zoned began to form and in February this year Belle typed the words Chapter One. And she fell in love.

With words.

With writing.

With a creative imagination she never knew she harbored.

Friend-Zoned is the first in the Friend-Zoned series. Keep an eye out for this cheeky author.

Belle has since published nine books including the *Friend-Zoned series, Willing Captive, the Night Fury serial, Raw, About Last Night* and *Lev*.

# About the Author
# Debra Anastasia

Debra Anastasia writes lies for a living. She can only cook chicken soup. In her house she has three dogs, one cat, two kids and a husband. It's like she runs a three-ring circus with one ring. You can find her at **DebraAnastasia.com** and on Twitter @Debra_Anastasia. But be prepared...

### Fire Down Below Excerpt

*Oh God. We're talking about me being naked, in the shower with cooter cream. Please world, end. Kill me.*

"I know it's not soap. I just... if it's scented... I can't do scented. Flowers and stuff like that. Fruit-flavored soaps make... things... burnish." She could tell from the peeks at his face Mr. Fitzwell had never stepped foot in bath and lotion store, wanting to try the array of fun fragrances. Nor had he purchased Peppermint Candy shower gel, foamed up his nether regions, and felt like he had dipped them in lava. Dove crossed and uncrossed her legs at the memory.

Mr. Fitzwell seemed concerned. "Okay, just a heads-up. It's definitely not good to put any fruits or plant life near your genitals." He made a V with his hands and formed his own pretend vagina in front of his pants.

Dove covered her eyes and tried to defend herself because now she could hear the sickly older woman beating her supporters with a purse.

Dove's mumbling got louder with her embarrassment. "I don't put weird things down... there. Just make sure that the cream's vagina-scented. Just plain. For vaginas." She kept her eyes on the counter.

## The Gynazule Series

Fire Down Below

Fire in the Hole

## Stand Alone

### The Revenger

### Excerpt from The Revenger

There was very little chatter after the alarming phone call. Savvy looked at the clock. It was only five, but the extra help Tallow had enlisted acted like she was about to disintegrate. When they were finally done, they hung Savvy's costume from a door, fully expecting her to drop trou in front of all the strangers.

She looked at the silver outfit meant to demean her and classify her as his, just like all his other favorites.

"Yeah, I'm not actually going to be wearing that." She looked from one shocked person to the other.

Tallow recovered first. "But this is what he told you to wear!"

Savvy laughed hollowly. "Yeah, he can suck his own dick for all I care."

The atmosphere changed. The others now realized Savvy didn't think it was a huge honor to be a fuckhole.

"That's not acceptable. I'll put you in it myself if I have to, but you're leaving here in that outfit." Tallow bravely gathered up the skirt and came into Savvy's personal space. He obviously thought she was just a regular girl.

In an instant she'd lifted Tallow into the air by his neck. "I'm not wearing it." She stared him down until he began to turn blue. Then she set him back on his feet.

Tallow was a quick learner and smoothed his fancy shirt. "Okay then, let me see what else we have."

### Other Books By Debra Anastasia

**The Poughkeepsie Brotherhood Series:**

Poughkeepsie Begins

Poughkeepsie

Enhanced Poughkeepsie

Return to Poughkeepsie

Saving Poughkeepsie

**The Seraphim Series**

Crushed Seraphim

Bittersweet Seraphim

**Novella:**

**Late Night with Andres**

**(100% of all proceeds donated to Save the Tatas)**

**Connect with Debra**

**Website:**
**www.DebraAnastasia.com**

Printed in Great Britain
by Amazon